PHILIP ALLAN
LITERATURE GUIDE

Philip Allan Updates, an imprint of Hodder Education, an Hachette UK company, Market Place, Deddington, Oxfordshire OX15 0SE

Orders
Bookpoint Ltd, 130 Milton Park, Abingdon, Oxfordshire OX14 4SB
tel: 01235 827827
fax: 01235 400401
e-mail: education@bookpoint.co.uk
Lines are open 9.00 a.m.–5.00 p.m., Monday to Saturday, with a 24-hour message answering service. You can also order through the Philip Allan Updates website: www.philipallan.co.uk

ISBN 978-1-4441-2141-4
First printed 2011

Impression number 5 4 3 2 1
Year 2016 2015 2014 2013 2012 2011

Cover photo reproduced by permission of Melvin Dockrey/Getty

Printed in Spain

Hachette UK's policy is to use papers that are natural, renewable and recyclable products and made from wood grown in sustainable forests. The logging and manufacturing processes are expected to conform to the environmental regulations of the country of origin.

P01787

Contents

Answers to the **Review your learning** questions are available online at: www.philipallan.co.uk/literatureguidesonline

Getting the most from this book and website

How to use this guide

You may find it useful to read sections of this guide when you need them, rather than reading it from start to finish. For example, you may find it helpful to read the *Plot and structure* section in conjunction with the novel, whether to back up your first reading of it at school or college or to help you revise. The *Tackling the assessments* section will be especially useful in the weeks leading up to the exam.

The following features have been used throughout this guide:

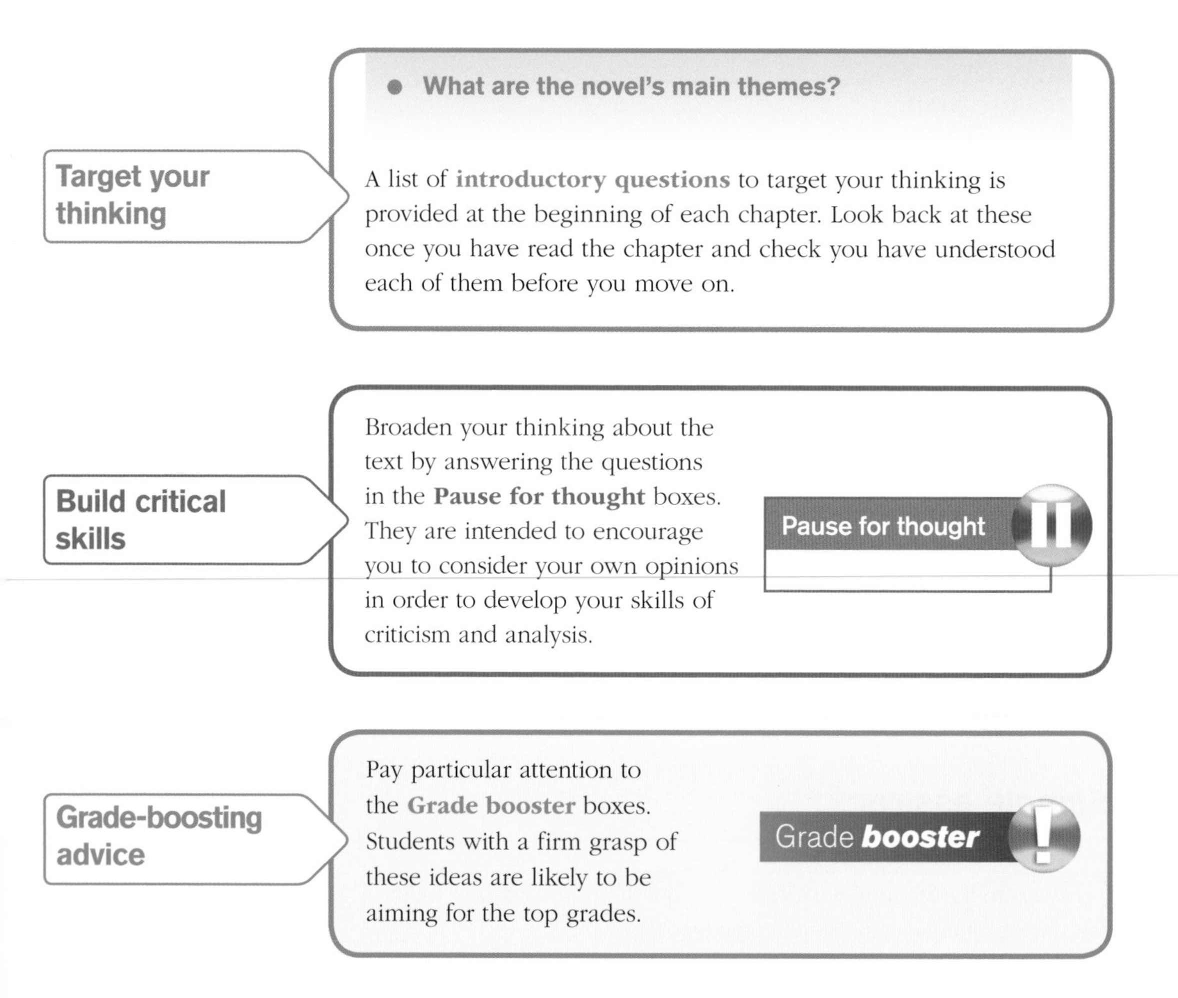

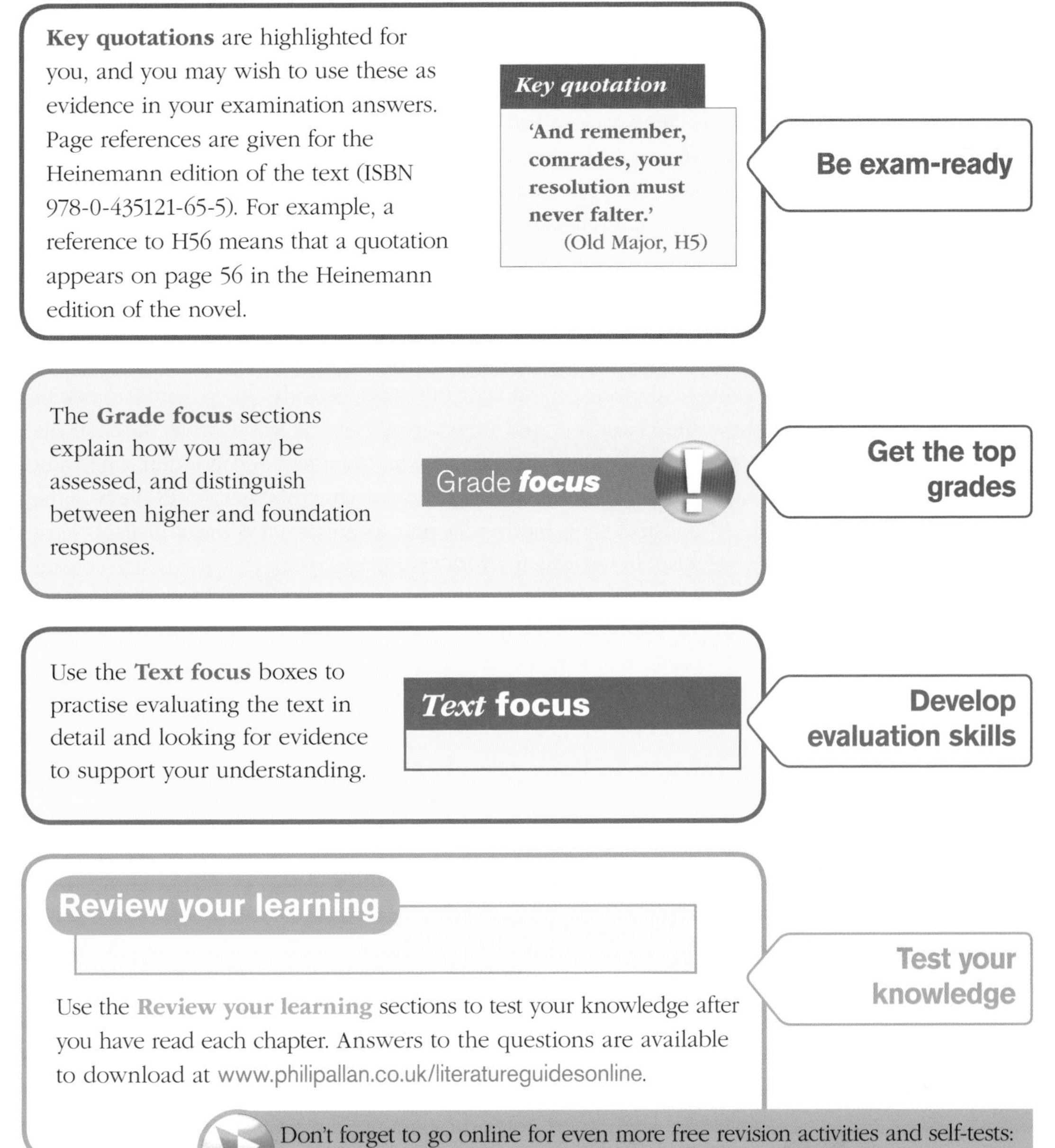

Key quotations are highlighted for you, and you may wish to use these as evidence in your examination answers. Page references are given for the Heinemann edition of the text (ISBN 978-0-435121-65-5). For example, a reference to H56 means that a quotation appears on page 56 in the Heinemann edition of the novel.

Key quotation

'And remember, comrades, your resolution must never falter.'
(Old Major, H5)

Be exam-ready

The **Grade focus** sections explain how you may be assessed, and distinguish between higher and foundation responses.

Grade ***focus***

Get the top grades

Use the **Text focus** boxes to practise evaluating the text in detail and looking for evidence to support your understanding.

***Text* focus**

Develop evaluation skills

Review your learning

Use the **Review your learning** sections to test your knowledge after you have read each chapter. Answers to the questions are available to download at www.philipallan.co.uk/literatureguidesonline.

Test your knowledge

Don't forget to go online for even more free revision activities and self-tests:
www.philipallan.co.uk/literatureguidesonline

Introduction

Approaching the text

A novel is, above all, a narrative. A large part of the storyteller's art is to make you want to find out what happens next, and therefore to keep you reading to the end. In order to study Animal Farm and to enjoy it, you need to keep a close track of the events that take place in it. This guide will help you to do that, but you may also benefit from keeping your own notes on the main events and who is involved in them.

However, any novel consists of much more than its events. You need to know the story well to get a good grade in the exam, but if you spend a lot of time simply retelling the story you will not get a high mark. You also need to keep track of a number of other features.

First, you need to take notice of the setting of the novel — where the events take place — and how this influences the story. You also need to know the characters and how Orwell lets us know what they are like. Notice how they are described, what they say and do, and what other characters say about them. Think about why they behave in the way they do — consider their motives — and what clues the writer gives us about these. Also, if you watch a film or stage adaptation of the novel, consider how characters are presented in this.

As you read on, you will notice themes: the ideas explored by the writer in the book. You may find it easier to think about these while not actually reading the novel, especially if you discuss them with other people. You should try to become aware of the style of the novel, especially on a second reading. This refers to how the writer presents the story. The context, background, to the book is also important.

All these aspects of the novel are dealt with in this guide. However, you should always try to notice them for yourself. This guide is no substitute for a careful and thoughtful reading of the text.

Grade *booster*

Make sure you know the novel. To achieve a top grade, reread the text before your assessment.

Revising the text

Animal Farm may be one of your English Literature set texts for examination or it could be one of the texts you use in a Controlled Assessment. In either case, knowing the text is essential. Making sure that you read the novel and keep good notes throughout your GCSE will help you; so too will proper revision and using this guide.

In your assessment, you may be allowed to use your text but it will have to be unannotated, so revision is really important.

It is a good idea to get the date of your exam or Controlled Assessment well in advance so that you can plan a revision timetable in the lead-up to the assessment. Give yourself plenty of time, especially if you have other subjects to revise for.

Grade ***booster***

Make sure you know all the key points very well (e.g. power is a major theme in the novel). Test yourself on these key points by talking about them, by writing them down without the help of your text or by planning responses to some questions in timed conditions.

Film and stage interpretations

There have been two film adaptations of *Animal Farm*: one produced in 1954 and another in 1999. The first — a cartoon animation — was Britain's first animated feature film and has received much attention as a result of this, along with revelations that its funding came from the CIA (Central Intelligence Agency), which wanted to fund anti-communist art. While it is heavily reliant on narration, the 1954 film is a landmark creation and includes a noted music score by Matyas Seiber and impressive vocal talents by Maurice Denham, who single-handedly provides every voice and animal noise in the film.

The 1999 film incorporates real actors alongside animals, aided by modern technology and digital animation. Neither film is entirely faithful to the original novel, with some changes to both events and characters, so if you do watch them, take care not to get confused. Nevertheless, both films are worth viewing in order to see how events and characters have been interpreted.

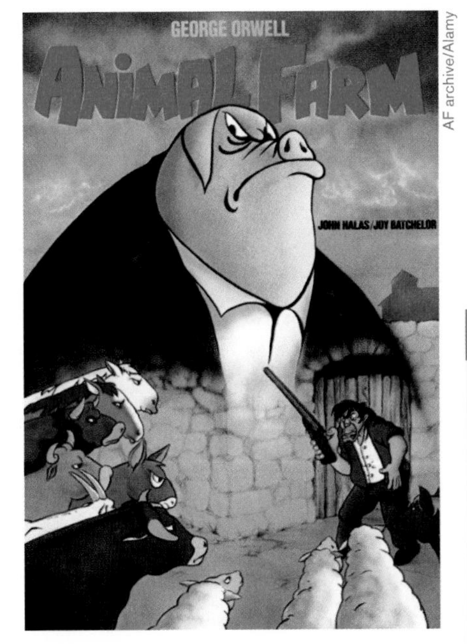

AF archive/Alamy

Poster advertising the release of the 1954 film version, with a central image of Napoleon, and Mr Jones to the right.

Alongside films of the novel, play scripts and stage adaptations exist, so it would be beneficial for you to keep an eye out for any local or national companies staging a production of *Animal Farm*. Ian Wooldridge and Peter Hall's play scripts of the novel offer an interesting comparison for you, and can be read quite easily alongside the original novel.

Grade ***booster***

The fact that to coincide with the film release in 1954 a comic strip serialisation of *Animal Farm*, illustrated by Harold Whitaker (one of the animators of the film) was also released in newspapers and other periodicals shows how important the novel was considered at the time.

Grade **booster**

Incorporating information about film or stage adaptations into your writing in a fluent and relevant way could get you extra marks. Adding this on as an after-thought or writing about interpretations as if they were what Orwell originally wrote will not. For example, saying that there are five commandments in the novel (which is what we see in the 1954 film) instead of seven (which is what we read in the book) will lose you marks.

Review your learning

(Answers available online)

1. Besides the story of the novel, what other aspects should you be aware of?
2. List two grade booster tips.
3. Why did the CIA fund the first film of *Animal Farm*?

More interactive questions and answers online.

Context

- **What does the term 'context' mean?**
- **What does the context of the novel tell us about its purpose?**
- **How did Orwell's experiences in life influence his novel?**
- **How does Orwell relate the events in the novel to those in the wider world?**

The context of a text refers to the circumstances at the time the text was written — in other words what was happening in society, the literary world and historically when *Animal Farm* was written. *Animal Farm* was written in 1945, the same year the Second World War ended, and five years before Orwell's death. Alongside *Nineteen Eighty-Four*, it is one of Orwell's most famous works, achieving the WH Smith and Penguin Books Great Reads of the Century award in 1995. Understanding the man behind the book, as well as political events in Britain and the world at the time the book was written, will help you to grasp the context of the novel.

Orwell's life

Early life and education

George Orwell's real name was Eric Arthur Blair. He was born in Motihari, India, in 1903. India was part of the British Empire at the time, and his father worked there as an agent in the Opium Department of the Indian Civil Service. Orwell came from a middle-class family — they led a relatively privileged life, though they were by no means rich.

When Orwell was eight years old, his family returned to England to live in Henley, though his father continued to work in India until 1912. His parents struggled to send him to a private prep school in Sussex and his experiences here, which he recounts in his autobiographical essay *Such, Such Were the Joys*, shaped his beliefs about the ease with which authority may be abused, which is reflected in his novel *Animal Farm*.

From here he gained a scholarship to Wellington, and then Eton, where he was taught French by Aldous Huxley, author of *Brave New World*. Orwell finished the final examinations at Eton but rather than attend either Oxford or Cambridge University, as many of his school fellows

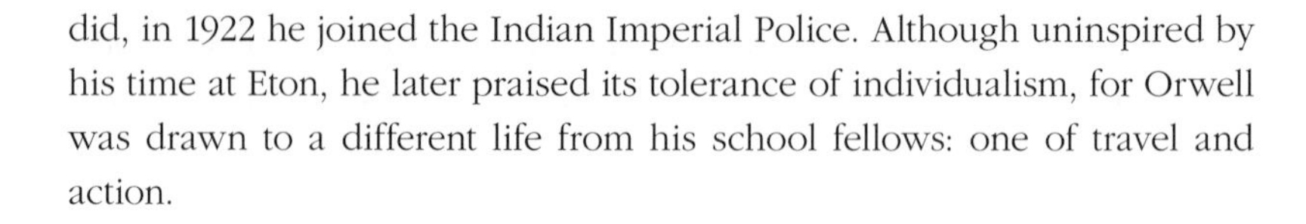

did, in 1922 he joined the Indian Imperial Police. Although uninspired by his time at Eton, he later praised its tolerance of individualism, for Orwell was drawn to a different life from his school fellows: one of travel and action.

Life as a writer

In 1927, Orwell resigned from the Imperial Police. He admitted that he was unsuited to life as a policeman. The life he really sought was to write; in fact, he had decided to become a writer at the age of five or six. This and his later disenchantment with the way Britain ruled India were early indications of his future as a political writer.

Orwell returned to England where he lived in a dingy bedroom in Portobello Road. Here, he started to teach himself how to write, working hours at a time. Then, in the spring of 1928, spurred on by the disgust and guilt he felt at his background and the imperialism of which he had been a part, he decided to live in poverty, in London and Paris. He worked as a dishwasher in Paris and then lived on the streets of London with tramps and among the poor. These experiences resulted in his book *Down and Out in Paris and London*, which was published in 1933. In this book, Orwell sought to educate the English middle class about the way in which the life they led and enjoyed was founded upon the exploitation of those whom they distanced themselves from. He viewed himself as part of the English moral conscience and his writings reflected this. (The way in which *Animal Farm* can be viewed as a moral tale is explored later in this guide.)

George Orwell on Walberswick Beach, Suffolk in 1934.

TopFoto

It was at this stage that Eric Arthur Blair took on the pseudonym George Orwell. Many have speculated about his reasons for doing this. Perhaps it was his way of shedding his old identity and taking on a new one. Eric Arthur Blair, middle-class student of Eton and English colonial policeman, became George Orwell, the classless anti-authoritarian writer.

However, unable to support himself with his writing, Orwell took up a teaching post at a private school before marrying Eileen O'Shaugnessy, a doctor's daughter, in 1936. In this same year, Orwell started to work as a shopkeeper in Wallington, Hertfordshire, and was later commissioned to produce a documentary account of unemployment in the north of England for the Left Book

Club, a left-wing organisation that sought to 'help in the struggle for world peace and against fascism.' *The Road to Wigan Pier* was published in 1937 and is viewed as a milestone in modern literary journalism, although the Left Book Club disliked Orwell's criticism in it of English attempts at socialism.

In *The Road to Wigan Pier*, Orwell writes of his desire to 'escape from… every form of man's dominion over man' and comments on the social structures that encourage 'dominion over others' — not just in relation to India but in connection with the English working class.

Spanish Civil War

Following publication of this non-fiction text, Orwell went to Spain in order to write newspaper articles on the Civil War, which was happening at the time. When Orwell arrived in Barcelona, he was surprised to find that what had seemed impossible in England was real in Spain. Class distinctions appeared to have vanished and while there was a shortage of everything, there *was* equality.

Socialism appeared to be a real possibility, something for which it was worth fighting, so Orwell joined in the struggle and was sent to the front in Aragon, near Zaragoza. However, when he returned to Barcelona a few months later, he found it had changed back to 'normal'. From his experiences in Spain, Orwell learned that socialism in action was a human possibility (if only temporary). However, it also confirmed for him that people cannot exist without different classes and that there is something in human nature that will always seek violence, conflict and power over others. His book *Homage to Catalonia* is an account of the civil war in Spain.

It became clear that while Orwell was a socialist, his experiences in life had led him to become disillusioned; when the fascism of Hitler and Mussolini was given the ironic title of 'national socialism', Orwell began to fear that socialism would have elements of fascism in it. This is seen in *Animal Farm* in the way that the socialist rebellion against the humans later gives way to a fascist dictatorship under the pigs.

Novel writing

In 1938, Orwell became ill with tuberculosis, so he spent the winter in Morocco where he wrote *Coming up for Air*, a novel that he published in 1939. In the same year, the Second World War started. Orwell was opposed to a war with Germany, but he condemned fascism. Wanting to fight, as he had done in Spain, Orwell tried to join the army but he was declared physically unfit.

He, therefore, served as a sergeant in the Home Guard and worked as a journalist for the BBC and the *Observer* and as literary editor for the *Tribune* during this time.

Towards the end of the war, Orwell wrote *Animal Farm: a fairy story*. The novel enjoyed great success, with large print runs despite the shortage of paper at the time in the UK and USA. Translated into many languages around the world, *Animal Farm* brought Orwell worldwide fame. It was also at this time that Orwell began to work as a reporter in Europe.

In 1944, he and his wife adopted a son, but sadly in 1945 his wife died during an operation. The following year Orwell went to the island of Jura in the Western Isles of Scotland, where he settled in 1946. This is where he wrote his famous novel *Nineteen Eighty-Four*. Unfortunately, the island's climate was unsuitable for someone suffering from tuberculosis and his novel reflects the gloom he felt while writing it.

In 1949, Orwell married Sonia Brownell but the marriage did not last long. Orwell died from tuberculosis in London University Hospital on 21 January 1950, soon after the publication of *Nineteen Eighty-Four* and shortly after his friend Desmond MacCarthy wrote to him saying, 'You have made an indelible mark on English literature...you are among the few memorable writers of your generation.'

Grade *booster*

Knowing about Orwell's background will help you to write more confidently about what influenced his writing of the novel.

Key terms

Term	Definition
Fascism	A governmental system led by a dictator who has complete power and who forcibly suppresses opposition and criticism, ensuring all industry, commerce etc. are centralised; usually emphasises an aggressive nationalism and often racism
Socialism	An economic system based on collective ownership (usually state ownership of money and industry)
Socialist	Someone who believes in socialism
Communism	A form of socialism that abolishes private ownership; all property is held in common, actual ownership being ascribed to the community as a whole or to the state
Communist	Someone who believes in communism
Left wing	Someone who is not closely bound to traditional ways and is supportive of government intervention to cure social problems
Anarchism	A theory or attitude that considers the state, as a compulsory government, to be unnecessary and favours the absence of the state (anti-government)
Anarchist	Someone who believes in anarchism

Spanish Civil War 18 July 1936–1 April 1939	This was a war in which the fascist Francisco Franco and his troops successfully seized control of Spain; a lot of different groups (including socialists, communists, anarchists and other left-wing groups) worked together with the Spanish Republic (the government at the time) to stop Franco. The fascist governments of Germany and Italy supplied troops and equipment to Franco, while the Soviet Union sold the Republican forces weapons; many people from other countries who did not like fascism volunteered to fight against Franco; these groups were known as the International Brigades but when the last of the Republican troops gave up, Franco became the ruler of Spain; he ruled his country until his death in 1975
Bolshevik	Left-wing majority group that followed Lenin; they eventually became the Russian Communist Party
Menshevik	Minority political group who expressed more moderate views than the Bolsheviks
Faction	Members of a group or organisation who hold views not representative of the group
Tsar	A male king or emperor
Autocracy	A form of government ruled by a single individual
Proletariat	Working class/lower class

The Soviet Union

The events in *Animal Farm* can be seen to relate to those in Russia between 1917 and 1941, therefore you need to know a bit of Russian history in order to discuss some of the novel's themes.

During the early part of the eighteenth century, Russia was ruled by tsars, who had ultimate authority under an imperial autocracy. Tsar Nicholas II ruled from 1894. Under his reign, the ruling classes lived in luxury while the rest of the population suffered, in the same way that, in the novel, Jones lives happily while the animals suffer. However, despite the desire for social and political change with minor revolts and the formation of political organisations, it was not until 1917 and the First World War's shortages and other hardships, that increased dissatisfaction and rebellion led to the February Revolution. In February 1917, the Bolsheviks forced Tsar Nicholas II to abdicate his position as leader of Russia. The nation's imperial rule under the Romanov dynasty ended, in a similar way to Jones being ousted from Manor Farm.

For more than half a year after the tsar's abdication, an ineffective provisional government ran Russia before Lenin (a Bolshevik leader) returned from exile and, helped by Leon Trotsky, another former exile, and Joseph Stalin, he launched a successful takeover against the provisional government. On 25 October 1917, a date known as the October

Revolution, a new government based on the tenets of communism was founded. In the same way, the animals in the novel establish a farm based on the ideals of 'Animalism'.

Although Lenin's New Economic Policy (NEP) increased agricultural production, his rise to power did not naturally lead to further success or popularity. Russia's former privileged classes as well as its working and farming classes became dissatisfied with the new government and as a result they started to garner foreign support for their cause. As a result, the White Army (aided by Britain and France) and the Red Army (led by Trotsky) were formed. In the novel, Jones's alliances with neighbouring farmers and the animals' battles against the humans, in particular the Battle of the Cowshed, mirror these events.

Lenin (left) and Stalin in 1922.

The Illustrated London News

Russia's Civil War lasted until 1921, and in 1922 the Union of Soviet Socialist Republics (USSR) was created. However, in 1924, Lenin, who had been leading the USSR, died. This left Trotsky and Stalin, both power-hungry politicians, to battle for Russia's leadership. In the same way, in the novel, Snowball and Napoleon are seen to battle over leadership of Animal Farm.

Despite Trotsky's ability as an orator, he was unable to defeat Stalin, who had the help of important internal alliances. Stalin expatriated Trotsky, along with many other leaders, in the Great Purge and eventually he had Trotsky assassinated in exile. For the next 25 years, Stalin was the leader of the Soviet Union. In a similar way, Napoleon exiles Snowball in order to rule the farm.

Russia suffered long-standing economic deficiencies and many losses as a result of the First World War, so in an effort to improve the situation,

Stalin abandoned NEP and launched several Five Year Plans — aggressive campaigns to increase the country's productivity while bringing the economy completely under government control. These ideas had originally been suggested by Trotsky in his efforts to industrialise Russia but had been dismissed by Stalin who had wanted to focus on building up defences. However, in an about-face, he now adopted these ideas. Similarly, Napoleon takes up Snowball's idea to build a windmill after initially ridiculing it.

These plans were successful but resulted in dissatisfaction among the citizens of the Soviet Union, particularly the kulaks, land-owning peasants who did not want their farms to be placed under government control. In order to prevent them from rebelling, Stalin used a carefully organised terror campaign. He began a series of 'purges' in which he killed anyone suspected of harbouring sentiments that went against his own. He was determined to protect himself and his government from treachery, so he increased the government's internal espionage, using the NKVD (the public and secret police organisation of the Soviet Union) and its subsidiary organisation, the KGB, and he turned Soviet citizens against one another.

Russian people were terrified of being imprisoned, tortured or sent to work in the Soviet labour camps. They also feared being executed, so they spied on and turned in their co-workers, neighbours and even family members. Tens of millions of people, many of whom were only *suspected* of being anti-Stalin, were slaughtered. This created a climate of fear in which Stalin had absolute control over Soviet society. Very similar events happen on Animal Farm: animals are seen to confess to crimes and are slaughtered as a result, and Napoleon controls the whole farm.

Stalin now focused his attention on international affairs. Feeling that Russia was isolated and at risk from outside forces, he joined the League of Nations in 1934 and after a failed attempt at joining an alliance against Hitler, Stalin signed a non-aggression pact with Germany in 1939. In *Animal Farm*, Napoleon's trading with Frederick mirrors this event. However, during the Second World War, Germany broke the non-aggression pact and invaded the Soviet Union. The war took a terrible toll on the Soviet Union and in 1943 Britain agreed to aid Russia against Hitler. Despite harsh battles and the loss of more than 20 million citizens, the Soviet Union managed to drive the Nazis out and continued marching westward, seizing control of Berlin in May 1945.

A few months later, George Orwell published *Animal Farm*, allegorically recounting much of this history. Stalin remained in control of the Soviet Union until he died in 1953.

Grade **booster**

Knowing that an allegory is a representation of something else will help you to describe the way in which Orwell represents Russian history in his novel.

Grade *focus*

You will not be assessed on context on its own, but you may get a question about how relevant the novel is today and some boards assess this in their Literature assessments (look at the Assessment Objectives section for details of AO4). It is the sign of a high-level candidate to be able to incorporate relevant contextual information into an essay in a constant and informed way. Writing one paragraph about context and then never mentioning it again will get you some marks but is the sign of someone working at the lower end of the grades. Use the table below to help you understand how, when writing about characters and events, you could incorporate context for different grades.

Grades A*–C	Grades D–G
Napoleon betrays the ideals of Animalism and starts to kill any animals on the farm who express anti-Napoleon sentiments, mirroring Stalin's purges in Russia when he staged 'show trials' in which people confessed to supposed crimes only to be publicly killed.	Napoleon becomes a dictator and kills animals on the farm.
The novel was written as an allegory to events in Russia and demonstrates Orwell's belief that while socialism is possible for a brief time, man will always seek power over others.	Events on the farm show the way in which people want power over each other.
The battle between Snowball and Napoleon symbolises the way that Trotsky and Stalin fought for control over Russia after Lenin's death.	Events in the book can be linked with Russian history. Napoleon and Snowball fight to control the farm but Napoleon wins.
Mr Jones represents the ruling class in Russia during the Romanov dynasty, in particular Tsar Nicholas II.	Mr Jones is a typical human wanting to boss the animals around. He is like the tsar in Russia.
Orwell was a disillusioned socialist who had seen the way in which ideals of equality could deteriorate into fascism. He used his experiences in life and in particular of the Spanish Civil War to highlight the fact that 'power corrupts and absolute power corrupts absolutely'.	Orwell used his experiences in life to write the novel as he thought socialism would always end badly.
Orwell subtitled his novel 'a fairy story', referring to the fictional nature of his book and its simple story line and language. However, his use of symbolism and direct prose make clear that his book is anything but a fairy tale; the novel is a satire and, unlike a fairy tale, there are no happy endings.	The book is called 'a fairy story' because it's all about animals and it's a simple story.

Review your learning

(Answers available online)

1. What does 'context' mean?
2. On what experiences did Orwell draw in writing *Animal Farm*?
3. Who in Russian history can we relate to Jones, Napoleon and Snowball?
4. Which event in history relates to Napoleon starting to trade with Frederick only to be conned by him later?

More interactive questions and answers online.

Plot and structure

- **What are the main events of the novel?**
- **How do the main storylines develop through the novel?**
- **How do these events correspond with Russian history?**

Chapter 1

- Manor farm is owned by Mr Jones, a drunken and negligent farmer.
- We are introduced to the farm animals.
- Old Major, the prize-winning boar, tells the animals about his dream, passing on his wisdom, which forms the basis of Animalism later in the novel.
- Old Major teaches the animals the song 'Beasts of England', which tells of a 'golden future time'.
- Jones hears the noise from the barn and fires his gun, causing the animals to disperse.

We are introduced to Mr Jones who is described in the first sentence as a neglectful farmer who drinks too much. Once he goes to sleep, the animals are described as 'stirring' and 'fluttering', suggesting the excitement of anticipation because old Major, the prize-winning white boar, has called a meeting in the barn in which he plans to tell the animals of his dream. Old Major is described as a well-respected pig and for this reason the animals are willing to lose some sleep over hearing his dream.

In the barn, we learn about main characters who will feature in the rest of the novel. We meet Boxer the cart-horse; Clover the motherly mare; Mollie the mare who pulls Jones's trap; Benjamin the donkey; Muriel the goat, and Moses the raven. Using carefully selected details, Orwell introduces us to these animals — some by breed, some by name — and we gain an impression of their characters from his descriptions.

Old Major talks about Man's tyranny over animals and suggests that animals are miserable and work as slaves, then are killed. He says that all they produce is taken by humans and that Man is the only enemy who tyrannises and consumes without producing. Old Major suggests that the only solution is rebellion against Man. He establishes that all men are enemies and all animals are comrades, and he goes on to describe an ideal future time when animals will live in freedom. He then says that the following rules, which later form the basis of Animalism, must be remembered:

Pause for thought

The animals on the farm have very different characteristics. Look at how Boxer, Clover and Benjamin are described. What impression do we gain of them and what do you think Orwell's allegorical purpose was in doing this?

- Animals must never resemble Man.
- Animals must never live in a house, lie in a bed, wear clothes, drink alcohol, use tobacco, touch money or engage in trade.
- No animal must tyrannise another.
- No animal must kill another.
- All animals are equal.

Pause for thought

Although old Major talks about animals being equal, there are early indications that they are not. Look at where the pigs sit when old Major speaks and at what happens between the rats and dogs at the end of old Major's speech. How does Orwell suggest existing power structures within the animal kingdom?

Old Major then teaches the animals a song called 'Beasts of England', which his mother had taught him and he remembered in his dream. The animals join in singing it. However, their singing wakes Jones, and we then see the tight grip he has on the animals; Jones's brutal response is to fire the gun which, Orwell cleverly points out, 'always stood in the corner of his bedroom', implying the violence with which Jones ruled his farm. The gun shot results in the animals' swift silence: 'the whole farm was asleep in a moment.'

Photos 12/Alamy

The animals sing 'Beasts of England', before Jones scares them to make them disperse.

Pause for thought

The song that the animals sing presents an idealised vision of the future. Consider the way in which the words in the song do this.

In this chapter Orwell sets the scene, introduces some key characters and establishes ideas that will inform the rest of the book.

Chapter 2

- Old Major dies and is buried.
- The pigs organise the Rebellion.
- We are introduced to Napoleon, Snowball and Squealer.

- Old Major's ideas are developed into a system known as 'Animalism'.
- Many animals do not understand its complex principles but Boxer and Clover are devoted to it and pass on their enthusiasm to others.
- Moses spreads rumours about 'Sugarcandy Mountain', undermining the pigs' teachings.
- After Jones forgets to feed the animals, the animals instigate the Rebellion.
- All signs of their slavery are destroyed, including Mollie's ribbons.
- The animals explore the farmhouse and agree that no animal should live there — it is to be a museum.
- Manor Farm's name is changed to 'Animal Farm'.
- The pigs reveal that they have taught themselves to write and Snowball, being the best writer, paints the Seven Commandments of Animalism on the barn.
- The pigs milk the cows and Snowball leads the animals out to make hay.
- When they return, the milk has disappeared and it is obvious that the pigs have drunk it.

Three nights later, old Major dies peacefully in his sleep. The animals secretly plot a rebellion, with the work of teaching and organising falling to the pigs, the most intelligent animals, and particularly to the two pigs Napoleon, a determined pig, and Snowball, a vivacious pig. Together with Squealer, another pig renowned for his talking prowess, they formulate the principles of Animalism, a philosophy based on old Major's teachings. They spread this among the other animals but many find the principles difficult to understand; they have grown up believing that Mr Jones is their rightful master.

Moses tempts animals with stories of 'Sugarcandy Mountain', an idyllic place situated in the sky. Many animals hate Moses for his tale telling and laziness but some believe in 'Sugarcandy mountain', a representation of Heaven, and the pigs work hard to dispel the myth of its existence.

We are told that although Mr Jones had been a 'capable farmer', he had always been a 'hard master'. With drink now, he had become neglectful. It is this neglect and the animals' lack of feeding that starts off a chain of events that leads to the unplanned rebellion.

The humans are shocked at 'the sudden uprising of creatures whom they were used to thrashing and maltreating just as they chose', so much so that it 'frightened them almost out of their wits'. They panic, take to their heels and are described as 'in full flight', with Mrs Jones hurriedly flinging a few possessions in a bag.

Pause for thought

It is clear that Mollie has early reservations about life without humans. What shows this?

Grade *booster*

Boxer and Clover are described as hard workers and loyal supporters of Animalism. Recognising that this heightens our reaction to the cruel way Boxer is treated later in the novel shows that you are aware of Orwell's authorial control.

Pause for thought

The animals are presented as victors. How does Orwell suggest this through his choice of words?

Once the humans are banished, the animals set to eliminating all reminders of Jones, and with all badges of slavery removed the animals are seen to rejoice, indulging in double rations and singing their anthem contentedly.

The next day, the animals wake up to a new dawn and, after surveying the farm, explore the farmhouse, from where Mollie takes a ribbon, only to be chastised by the others. The animals decide that no animal shall ever live in the farmhouse and that it should be preserved as a museum.

After breakfast, the pigs tell the others that they have taught themselves to write. Snowball writes the new name of the farm, 'Animal Farm' in place of Manor Farm, and with Squealer's help he writes the principles of Animalism which the pigs have reduced to seven 'unalterable' commandments. They state:

- Whatever goes upon two legs is an enemy.
- Whatever goes upon four legs, or has wings, is a friend.
- No animal shall wear clothes.
- No animal shall sleep in a bed.
- No animal shall drink alcohol.
- No animal shall kill any other animal.
- All animals are equal.

Snowball paints the Animals' commandments on the barn wall.

Photos 12/Alamy

Shortly afterwards, it becomes apparent that the cows need to be milked. This the pigs manage to do and despite concerns over what will happen to the milk, Napoleon tells the others to follow Snowball to harvest, for them only to return to find the milk has disappeared.

The interval between old Major's death and the Rebellion signifies the long period in history when socialism grew. Following the death of Marx and Engels, political ideas developed and the working classes grew more educated and started to want more from life.

Orwell develops our understanding of the three main pigs in this chapter and draws distinctions between all the animals' views of the new system. He also introduces the idea of organised religion through Moses and indicates the suspicious way it is viewed. This is in keeping with Marx's view that organised religion was an 'opiate of the masses' that prevented people from changing their lives for the better.

At the end of the chapter Orwell indicates the way in which ideals will be broken.

Grade **booster**

Knowing how events in *Animal Farm* correlate with real history will gain you marks.

Chapter 3

- The animals work hard and the harvest is successful.
- The pigs assume leadership.
- Boxer devotes himself to the Rebellion.
- Mollie continually shirks work.
- Every Sunday, the animals meet and raise the flag.
- Disagreements between Napoleon and Snowball become apparent.
- Snowball is concerned with education for all, and most animals become literate to some degree.
- 'Four legs good, two legs bad' is the new maxim that Snowball creates to help the less intelligent animals understand the Seven Commandments.
- Napoleon takes a greater interest in educating the young rather than old.
- He removes the dogs' puppies.
- Squealer persuades the other animals that the pigs are 'brain workers' and therefore need the apples and milk.
- He suggests that if the animals disagree, the pigs could fail and Jones would return.

The animals work very hard and, despite using instruments created for humans, the harvest is completed in two days less than it had taken Jones and his men and is the biggest the farm has seen.

The pigs do not work but direct others, assuming leadership of the farm. In contrast, Boxer gets up earlier than the others and works harder than ever, adopting the motto of 'I will work harder' when faced with difficulties. Meanwhile, the cat and Mollie shirk work and Benjamin remains his cynical self.

Grade **booster**

Knowing the way in which *Animal Farm*'s flag, with its images of animal parts, is similar to the Red Banner that the Bolsheviks used as a symbol of their ideological commitment to placing all authority in the hands of workers and peasants, will gain you extra marks in an exam.

Pause for thought

Consider why Napoleon focuses on educating the young and his reasons for taking the puppies.

Grade **booster**

Recognising that Squealer's manipulation represents political rhetoric — the indoctrination of the uneducated — shows that you understand how the novel is satirical.

On Sundays, there is no work, breakfast is an hour later and the animals meet for a ceremony involving the hoisting of a flag — a green tablecloth with a hoof and horn painted on it — and a meeting in the barn, where the forthcoming week is discussed.

The pigs make resolutions but Snowball and Napoleon constantly disagree. It is agreed, however, that the small paddock behind the orchard should be a resting place for retiring animals, although Snowball and Napoleon fail to agree on a retiring age.

Snowball sets up a number of Animal Committees, most of which fail. However, his educational initiatives prove successful, with most animals gaining some degree of literacy. Benjamin learns to read as well as the pigs but Boxer cannot get beyond the letter D in the alphabet. To make things easier, Snowball simplifies the Seven Commandments to 'Four legs good, two legs bad' for the less intelligent animals, and the sheep learn and repeat this maxim for hours on end.

Napoleon takes no interest in Snowball's committees, seeing education of the young as a priority. He takes Jessie and Bluebell's nine puppies saying that he will take responsibility for their education and installs them in the loft, which is inaccessible to others.

Later, it is revealed that the milk is being mixed into the pigs' mash, and when the apples ripen they too are taken to the harness room for the pigs' use. Squealer explains to the other animals that milk and apples are necessary for pigs because they are 'brain workers' and he suggests that without them the pigs could fail in protecting the animals from the return of Mr Jones. All the animals agree that this would be a bad thing.

In this chapter, Orwell develops our understanding of the differences between Snowball and Napoleon. Snowball busies himself with organising the work of the farm while Napoleon starts to develop his power base, looking towards the future when he will use the dogs to secure his control. This parallels the contrast between Trotsky and Stalin, with Trotsky focusing on organising Workers' Committees to educate the illiterate Russian masses and teach them about Communism and Stalin establishing his power base. Squealer's role as the voice of media and propaganda is also established in this chapter.

Chapter 4

- News of the Rebellion spreads across half the county and pigeons from Animal Farm teach 'Beasts of England' to animals on neighbouring farms.
- The two neighbouring farmers, Mr Pilkington and Mr Frederick, are always on bad terms.

- Mr Pilkington and Mr Frederick fear the Rebellion and spread false rumours about Animal Farm.
- In October, Jones is helped by Frederick and Pilkington to attack the farm.
- Snowball leads the animals to victory in what becomes known as the Battle of the Cowshed.
- Napoleon is conspicuous by his absence.
- Boxer and Snowball are awarded medals for bravery.

By late summer, news of the Rebellion has spread across half the county. Mr Jones spends most of his time in the Red Lion Pub drinking and complaining about his misfortune. His neighbours, Mr Pilkington of Foxwood Farm and Mr Frederick of Pinchfield Farm, fear their own animals will follow those on Manor Farm but their rivalry with each other prevents them from working together against Animal Farm. Instead, they refuse to recognise Animal Farm's name and spread false rumours about the farm's inefficiency and immorality. Meanwhile, pigeons sent by Napoleon and Snowball spread news of the Rebellion and teach animals 'Beasts of England', so that many begin to behave rebelliously.

Finally, in early October, Mr Jones and some of Pilkington's and Frederick's men attempt to seize control of Animal Farm. A flight of pigeons alerts the other animals of this and Snowball, who has studied books about the battle campaigns of Julius Caesar, leads the animals in an ambush. Boxer and Snowball fight courageously and the humans are ejected quickly with victory falling to the animals.

The animals lose only a sheep, who is given a hero's burial. Thinking that he has unintentionally killed a stable boy who is later discovered to have fled, Boxer expresses his regret at taking a life. However, Snowball reassures him not to feel guilty, stating that 'the only good human being is a dead one.'

Mollie's ability to shirk is seen again as she is found hiding in her stall after the battle. Snowball and Boxer each receive medals inscribed with the words 'Animal Hero, First Class'. The animals decide to call the battle the 'Battle of the Cowshed', and after discovering Mr Jones's gun where he dropped it in the mud, they place this at the base of the flagstaff, agreeing to fire it twice a year: on 12 October, the anniversary of the battle, and on Midsummer's Day, the anniversary of the Rebellion.

In this chapter, Orwell draws parallels between the attempt by the pigs to spread Animalism and the efforts of early followers of Communism to spread its ideas. Just as the West refused to cooperate politically with the USSR, in this chapter Pilkington and Frederick refuse to recognise Animal Farm. Also, the West's financial and military aid to the White Army — old

Grade *booster*

Linking the humans' attempts to regain the farm with the counter-revolution in Russia when the White Army, helped by Britain and France, invaded Russia but were defeated by the Trotsky-led Red Army, will show that you understand the novel in context.

supporters of the tsarist regime — is symbolised by Orwell in the Battle of the Cowshed. The higher status assumed by the pigs in terms of rations indicates the way in which ideals are being broken.

Chapter 5

- Mollie disappears and is never spoken of again.
- Snowball and Napoleon continue to disagree.
- Snowball proposes the building of a windmill to improve conditions on the farm but Napoleon sees security as a top priority.
- The animals are divided until a rousing speech by Snowball convinces them to vote for the windmill.
- Snowball is chased off the farm by dogs that Napoleon has secretly trained.
- Napoleon announces the end to Sunday meetings and democratic votes; a committee of pigs will make all decisions now.
- Squealer tells the animals that the windmill will be built after all and that Napoleon never really opposed it.

As winter draws on, it becomes apparent that Mollie has become more and more difficult. She arrives late for work, accepts treats from men linked with nearby farms, and generally behaves in a way contrary to the principles of Animalism. Eventually she disappears and the pigeons later report that she has been lured away by a fat, red-faced man who strokes her coat and feeds her sugar and that she now pulls his carriage. None of the other animals ever mentions Mollie again.

> **Pause for thought**
>
> What reasons might the animals have for never mentioning Mollie again?

During the cold winter months, the animals continue to hold their meetings in the barn, and Snowball and Napoleon continue to disagree over issues. It is evident that Snowball is the better speaker, but Napoleon is better at gaining support in between meetings.

Snowball is ambitious for the farm. He studies Mr Jones's books and is full of ideas for making improvements. One of these includes a scheme to build a windmill, from which the animals can generate electricity, thus reducing the burden on them. However, Napoleon asserts that building the windmill will entail a lot of hard work and difficulty and that the animals should attend to their immediate needs rather than plan for a distant future. He places greater importance on securing the farm by procuring firearms and training animals to use them. The animals are divided but in an act of contempt, Napoleon surveys Snowball's initial plans and urinates on them.

When Snowball's windmill plans are finalised, all the animals assemble for a great meeting to vote whether to carry out the project. Snowball gives a powerful speech, but Napoleon's response is just thirty seconds long and dismissive. When Snowball speaks further, inspiring the animals with his descriptions of the wonders of electricity, the animals are moved to side with him, but just as they prepare to vote, Napoleon gives a strange whimper and nine enormous dogs charge into the barn. They attack Snowball, chasing him off the farm.

When the dogs return to their master's side, Napoleon announces that henceforth meetings will only be held for ceremonial purposes. All important decisions will fall to the pigs.

Many of the animals feel confused and disturbed by these events but Squealer placates them; he explains that Napoleon is making a great sacrifice in taking responsibility for leadership and that, as the cleverest animal, he serves the interests of all of them. The animals still question the expulsion of Snowball but Squealer explains that Snowball was a traitor and a criminal and, despite initial reservations, eventually, the animals come to accept this version of events, especially when they are told that Jones may return. Boxer adds 'Napoleon is always right' to his other motto 'I will work harder'.

In Sunday meetings now, Napoleon and the other pigs take to sitting on a raised platform from where they issue their orders. Three weeks after Snowball's banishment, the animals learn that Napoleon, in fact, supports the windmill project. Squealer explains that he never really opposed it. He just pretended to in order to expel the disloyal Snowball. These tactics, according to Squealer, served to advance the interest of all the animals. Squealer's words, combined with the threatening growls of his three dogs, convince the animals to accept his explanation without question.

In this chapter, Mollie represents those Russians who defected to the West in search of a better life and more personal freedom. Also in this chapter, Orwell draws parallels between Napoleon and Snowball's differences and Stalin and Trotsky's disagreements over organisation

Pause for thought

Propaganda is defined as 'the deliberate spreading of ideas or information, true or untrue, with the purpose of manipulating public opinion to gain support for one's cause or to discourage support for another'. Squealer acts as the voice of propaganda. Find examples of how he does this in this chapter.

RIA Novosti/TopFoto

Russian propaganda poster from 1918 with the slogan 'We will win!'

Pause for thought

In the novel, which animals represent the secret police?

and industrial development. Stalin wanted to make Russia as powerful and advanced as the West and drove Trotsky out of Russia, helped by the OGPU (the Russian secret police).

Minimus's inclusion indicates the way that Communist Russia used art and literature to promote its values. The rewriting of history begins in this chapter, with Squealer stating that Napoleon was never against the windmill.

Chapter 6

- The animals work a 60-hour week and Sunday work is introduced.
- Building of the windmill proves difficult.
- Napoleon announces that the animals will trade with neighbouring farms to help finance the windmill and he has engaged a solicitor to mediate.
- Squealer placates the animals' unease.
- The pigs move into the farmhouse, sleep in beds and get up an hour later than the other animals.
- The Fourth Commandment is changed to justify the pigs sleeping in beds, and Squealer persuades the animals using fear of Jones's return.
- The windmill is destroyed in a storm and Snowball is blamed.

The animals work like slaves doing a 60-hour week. In August, Napoleon announces that the animals are also to work on Sunday afternoons. While this work is 'voluntary', animals will receive no food unless they carry it out.

The animals are loyal to the farm and believe what the pigs tell them so they commit themselves to the extra work. Boxer, in particular, toils very hard, doing the work of three horses but never complaining. Despite having all the necessary material to build the windmill, the animals face a number of difficulties. As they are unable to use picks and crowbars, they struggle to break the stone into usable sizes to build the windmill. However, once they learn to raise and then drop big stones into the quarry, they succeed in smashing them into easier chunks and finally solve this problem. By late summer, they have enough broken stone to begin construction.

Although the animals' work is exhausting, they do not suffer any more than they had done under Mr Jones. They have enough to eat and can maintain the farm grounds easily now that humans no longer take their produce. However, the farm still needs items that it cannot produce on site, such as iron, nails and paraffin oil. When existing supplies of these begin to run low, Napoleon announces a new policy of trading with neighbouring farms. Despite some animals' misgivings and vague recollections that they had agreed not to do this, the dogs' growling and Napoleon's reassurances that all arrangements have been made, along with Squealer's talks afterwards, make the animals believe they are mistaken.

Mr Whymper, a human solicitor, is hired to assist Napoleon in conducting trade on behalf of Animal Farm. He begins to visit the farm every Monday, and Napoleon places orders with him for various supplies.

The pigs start to live in the farmhouse and it is rumoured that they sleep in beds, a violation of the Fourth Commandment. However, when Clover asks Muriel to read her the commandment, they find that it now reads 'No animal shall sleep in a bed *with sheets*.'

Pause for thought

How does Squealer allay the animals' fears about engaging in trade with humans?

According to Squealer, Clover must have forgotten the last two words. He assures the animals that a pile of straw is a bed and that they all therefore sleep in beds. Sheets, as a human invention, are the true source of evil. He emotionally blackmails the animals into agreeing that the pigs need proper rest in order to think clearly and serve the best interests of the farm.

In November, a terrible storm hits Animal Farm, knocking down, among other things, the windmill. The animals are devastated but Napoleon blames this on Snowball, who, he says, will do anything to destroy Animal Farm. He passes a death sentence on Snowball, offering a bushel of apples to anyone who kills him. He then gives an impassioned speech in which he convinces the animals that they must rebuild the windmill. His parting words are, 'Long live the windmill! Long live Animal Farm!'

In this chapter, Orwell draws a parallel between the building of the windmill and Stalin's first Five Year Plan. The struggles that the animals face represent the difficulties faced by Russia in developing as an industrial nation. We see in this chapter the power and control that the pigs now have over the animals. Orwell suggests the slow deterioration in conditions, with the animals being treated as they were in Jones's time. Things begin to return to what they once were: the farm trades and the pigs start to become the elite, moving in to the farmhouse. Fear is seen as a control mechanism, just as it was in Communist Russia; Squealer always has the dogs with him when trying to persuade the animals. This is the first chapter in which a commandment is changed.

Chapter 7

- Conditions and morale worsen as the animals face starvation.
- Work on the windmill is slow.
- Napoleon tricks Whymper into thinking that rumours of famine are false.

- Napoleon announces that the hens must surrender their eggs for trade, and when they rebel he starves them out.
- Rumours about Snowball's treachery are spread and he becomes a scapegoat for all that goes wrong.
- Napoleon calls a meeting during which the dogs attack Boxer but are rebuffed.
- Four pigs and three hens, alongside other animals, confess crimes and are killed in a series of purges. The other animals are stunned.
- Clover thinks about the ideals of Animal Farm and leads the animals in singing 'Beasts of England' only to be told by Squealer that this is no longer an appropriate song.
- A new, less satisfying song is introduced.

The winter is bitter. Snow, sleet and frost hamper the animals as they struggle to rebuild the windmill. The humans refuse to believe that Snowball was behind the destruction of the windmill, claiming that the windmill's walls were not thick enough. Despite stating that this is false, the animals decide to build the windmill walls twice as thick.

When the animals fall short of food in January and face possible starvation, rumours of famine and disease spread. To counter this, Napoleon has Mr Whymper visit the farm and tricks him into thinking rations have been increased and grain stores are full.

However, to feed the animals, Napoleon decides to sell 400 eggs a week. The animals are shocked, believing that one of old Major's original complaints against humans centred on the cruelty of egg selling, but when the hens rebel, smashing their eggs, Napoleon starves them out, cutting their rations entirely. Nine hens die before the others submit to Napoleon's demands.

Pause for thought

Part of Napoleon's tactics is to use Squealer to spread false rumours about Snowball and rewrite history. How does he do this in the spring?

The animals are astonished at what Squealer says about Snowball, especially Boxer who is completely bemused, recalling the medal Snowball was given. However, Squealer describes events so vividly, claiming Napoleon to have been the hero at the Battle of the Cowshed, and that Napoleon has said 'categorically that Snowball was Jones's agent from the very beginning' that even Boxer finally agrees to this version of events.

Pause for thought

How does Orwell signify at this point that something might happen to Boxer later?

Four days later, Napoleon calls all the animals into the yard. With his dogs around him, he forces specific animals to confess their participation in a conspiracy with Snowball. The dogs tear out the throats of these 'traitors' and then, seemingly without orders, they attack Boxer, who effortlessly kicks them away with his hooves. Four pigs and various other animals are killed, including the hens who rebelled against selling their eggs.

The animals are deeply upset and confused by these events. Once Napoleon leaves, Boxer states that he cannot believe that such a thing could happen on Animal Farm and he thinks that it must result from some fault in the animals. He, therefore, commits to working even harder. Clover on the other hand wonders how their glorious Rebellion could have come to this.

When Clover leads some of the animals to sing 'Beasts of England', Squealer appears and explains that 'Beasts of England' is no longer to be sung as it is the song of the Rebellion and now that there is no more need for rebellion, the song is defunct. Squealer presents the animals with a replacement song, written by Minimus, the poet pig, which expresses patriotism and glorifies Animal Farm but does not inspire the animals as much.

In this chapter, Orwell shows how Snowball, like Trotsky, becomes the scapegoat who is blamed for everything and is accused of industrial sabotage. The rewriting of history continues in this chapter, with Snowball's acts in the Battle of the Cowshed being altered. The confessions by the animals are akin to those expressed in the 1930s in the USSR when Stalin set about removing anyone who appeared to oppose him.

When Clover thinks back to the past, Orwell reminds us of the ideals that have been shattered. This is reinforced when the anthem of rebellion is replaced with a less satisfying song.

Grade *booster*

Between 1934 and 1938, seven million Russians were executed or put into labour camps. Knowing that the killing of animals in Chapter 7 represents these purges will gain you additional marks.

Chapter 8

- The Sixth Commandment has been changed to justify the killing of the animals.
- The animals are working harder and eating less than in Jones's time but Squealer uses statistics to convince the animals that they are better off.
- Napoleon increasingly assumes emperor status.
- Napoleon is negotiating the sale of some timber to either Pilkington or Frederick.
- The reconstruction of the windmill is completed.
- The wood is sold to Frederick who tricks the animals by paying in forged notes.
- Frederick and his men attack the farm, blowing up the windmill in the 'Battle of the Windmill'.
- The animals suffer great losses but Napoleon declares it a victory as the farm is not lost.
- The pigs break the Fifth and Third Commandments when they get drunk on some whisky and Napoleon emerges wearing a hat.
- When Napoleon has a hangover, it is announced that he is dying but he recovers and later the Fifth Commandment is changed.

A few days after the trauma of the executions, the animals discover that the Sixth Commandment reads: 'No animal shall kill any other animal *without cause*.' Once again, the animals blame this apparent change in wording on their bad memories. They work even harder to rebuild the windmill and although they suffer from hunger and cold, Squealer continually blinds them with science, citing statistics to prove that conditions on the farm are better than what they experienced under Mr Jones and that they continue to improve.

Pause for thought

Look back at old Major's speech. How does Napoleon's behaviour contravene what he said?

Napoleon is rarely seen and, when he is, he is surrounded by dogs and his presence is announced by a cockerel. He adopts the title of 'Leader' along with other complimentary names. Minimus writes a poem in praise of Napoleon and inscribes it on the barn wall.

It is at this time that Napoleon enters complicated negotiations to sell some timber. The pigs incite hatred of whoever appears not to be buying the timber at the time. They encourage the animals to hate Pilkington when negotiations favour Frederick, and vice versa. Snowball is also said to be hiding in whichever farm is currently out of favour. Following great anti-Frederick propaganda during which Napoleon promotes the maxim 'Death to Frederick!', the animals are shocked to learn that Frederick is the final buyer of timber. Napoleon's cleverness is endlessly praised by the pigs, for, rather than accept a cheque for the timber, he insists on receiving cash, which he gets in the form of five pound notes.

Soon the windmill is finished but before they can put it to use, Napoleon discovers that the money Frederick has given him for the timber is fake. Napoleon pronounces the death sentence on Frederick and warns the animals to prepare themselves for the worst.

Soon Frederick attacks Animal Farm, aided by a large group of armed men. Frederick's men use dynamite to blow up the windmill. In response, the enraged animals attack the men, driving them away, but suffering heavy casualties; several animals are killed and Boxer sustains a serious injury. The animals feel dejected, but after a patriotic flag-raising ceremony their faith is somewhat restored.

Pause for thought

Look at page 68. Find elements that show that Napoleon's actions are inconsistent as a result of his drinking alcohol.

A few days later, the pigs discover a crate of whisky in the farmhouse cellar and that night, the animals hear singing and commotion and spot Napoleon wearing Mr Jones's old bowler hat. The next morning, the pigs look bleary-eyed and sick, and Squealer emerges to tell the others that Comrade Napoleon is dying. A rumour that Snowball has poisoned him circulates but by evening, Napoleon has recovered.

The next night, some of the animals are woken by a noise that turns out to be Squealer, who has fallen off a ladder. Nearby are an overturned paint pot and a paint-brush. Only Benjamin understands, but he says nothing.

A few days later, the animals discover that the Seventh Commandment now reads, 'No animal shall drink alcohol *to excess*,' but once again they blame their memories for remembering the commandment wrongly.

In this chapter, Orwell shows the gradual erosion of ideals when Napoleon adopts various titles and has a food taster, suggesting the emperor-like status he now holds. Further, Napoleon's complex negotiations with neighbouring farmers mirror the attempts by Stalin to broker a deal with Western democracies, and the sale of timber to Frederick is akin to Stalin's pact with Adolf Hitler. Orwell also uses the deception of the forged notes to indicate the way in which Russia was deceived when Germany attacked it in 1941. The Battle of the Windmill in the novel represents the Battle of Stalingrad, a turning point for Russia, when the Russians drove the invading German army out of Russia, though suffering huge casualties in the process. In this chapter, Orwell shows the way in which the pigs' breaking of rules signifies the continuing loss of ideals.

Chapter 9

- Boxer's hoof takes a long time to heal but he looks forward to his retirement.
- All rations are reduced except for the pigs' and dogs'.
- Young pigs are to be educated separately in a schoolroom built by the other animals.
- Barley is used not in animal feed but to brew beer.
- Animal Farm becomes a republic, with Napoleon as president.
- Further rumours about Snowball's treachery are spread.
- Moses returns to the farm and spreads his tales of Sugarcandy Mountain, which some animals take comfort in.
- Boxer collapses and is sold by the pigs to the knacker's yard, although the pigs convince the animals that he went to the vet's.
- A crate of whisky appears and the pigs have a party.

Life is hard, with rations reduced again in December for all animals, except the pigs and dogs, although Squealer explains this away. Talk of animals retiring circulates, although none has. Boxer's twelfth birthday — the age of retirement for horses — is approaching and his hoof, which was injured in battle, is giving him trouble. Both Clover and Benjamin tell him to work less hard but he does not listen. His only goal is to see the windmill off to a good start before he retires. He looks forward to a comfortable life in the pasture as a reward for his lifetime of hard work.

When four sows give birth to 31 piebald piglets, Napoleon is assumed the father. He commands that a schoolroom be built for their education.

Pause for thought

What else in this chapter shows the way pigs are being treated as privileged members of the farm?

Stocks run low and rations reduce again in February. Trade increases. Napoleon begins ordering events called 'Spontaneous Demonstrations', where the animals march around the farm, listen to speeches and take pride in the glory of Animal Farm. When a few animals complain about the wasted time and cold this entails, the sheep, who love these Demonstrations, drown them out with bleats of 'Four legs good, two legs bad!'

In April, Animal Farm becomes a republic, and Napoleon, the sole candidate for leadership, takes on the role of president in a unanimous vote. The same day, documents revealing Snowball's complicity with Jones at the Battle of the Cowshed are revealed. It is now said that Snowball openly fought with Jones and cried 'Long live Humanity!', his injuries having been caused by Napoleon's teeth. Because the battle occurred so long ago, the animals accept this new story.

Pause for thought

Although the pigs officially condemn these stories, they allow Moses to live on the farm without requiring him to work and give him beer. Why do you think this is?

In the middle of the summer, Moses the raven returns to the farm and begins to spread his stories about Sugarcandy Mountain.

The animals continue to work like slaves, rebuilding the windmill and erecting the new schoolroom. Even though his hoof has healed and he continues to work hard, Boxer's appearance changes — his hide is less shiny and his haunches shrunken. One day, Boxer collapses while pulling stone for the windmill. The other animals rush to tell Squealer, while Benjamin and Clover stay by his side.

Squealer announces that Napoleon has arranged that Boxer will be treated in Willingdon at a human hospital to recuperate. However, when the van arrives, a few days later, Benjamin reads the writing on the side and announces that Boxer is being sent to a glue maker to be slaughtered. The animals panic and start to call out to Boxer to escape. Then they hear him kicking feebly inside the van, but he is unable to get out.

Three days later, Squealer announces that Boxer has died in hospital. Claiming to have been at Boxer's side when he died, he talks of how moved he was and says that Boxer died praising the glories of Animal Farm. Squealer condemns the false rumours that Boxer was taken to a glue factory, and allays the animals' fears by telling them that the hospital had bought the van from a glue maker and had failed to paint over the van's lettering. The animals are relieved at this, and when Napoleon gives a speech in praise of Boxer, on the following Sunday, they feel completely placated.

Pause for thought

Where has the money come from?

Shortly afterwards, the farmhouse receives a delivery from the grocer and sounds of partying erupt from within. It becomes apparent that the pigs have found the money to buy another crate of whisky — though no one knows where they have acquired the money.

In this chapter, Orwell makes clear the great distance between the pigs and the other animals. The way in which propaganda is used is emphasised through Squealer here and Orwell makes clever use of Moses in this chapter to signify the way in which the pigs openly condemn his tales but use them to pacify the animals. This represents the way in which Stalin initially persecuted the Church, but did a complete U-turn towards religious tolerance when he needed to use it to support his failing power base against the Nazis of Germany. This chapter is significant in that Boxer dies and is sold and the farm's status changes to a republic with Napoleon as president. Both these incidents signal a complete betrayal of ideals.

Chapter 10

- Many years pass; animals die but none ever retires.
- Few of the younger animals understand Animalism.
- The farm is rich but the animals are not.
- The animals are content knowing they live in equality.
- Clover is horrified to see the pigs walk on two legs contrary to the First Commandment.
- Napoleon emerges with a whip.
- The Seven Commandments have been replaced by just one, the Seventh, which now reads: 'All animals are equal but some animals are more equal than others.'
- Napoleon and the other pigs take on the habits of humans.
- They invite the other farmers to dinner, where an argument breaks out.
- The animals watch through the window and cannot tell the difference between the humans and the pigs.

Years pass. Many animals age and die. Only Clover, Benjamin, Moses and a few pigs recall the days before the Rebellion. The farm is now organised and prosperous, with two additional fields having been bought from Pilkington. The windmill has been completed but is not used for generating electricity. Instead, corn is milled, providing the farm with much profit. Another windmill is being built but the luxuries Snowball talked of are denounced by Napoleon who says Animalism is about hard work and frugal living.

Meanwhile the farm seems to have grown richer, with only the pigs and dogs living comfortably. Squealer explains that the pigs and dogs do important work — filling out forms and carrying out administrative tasks. Mostly, the other animals accept this explanation and their lives continue as before. Despite the hardships they endure, they never lose their sense

of pride in Animal Farm. They still believe passionately in the goals of the Rebellion — a world free from human tyranny, where all animals are equal.

One day, Squealer leads the sheep off to a remote spot to teach them a new song. Shortly afterwards, when the animals have just finished their day's work, they hear the horrified neighing of Clover, who summons the others to the yard. There, they find Squealer walking on his hind legs. Several other pigs follow suit before Napoleon emerges from the farmhouse on his hind legs and carrying a whip.

Pause for thought

Look carefully at page 84. How does Orwell make clear the significance of this moment?

Grade *booster*

Knowing that this is a key moment in the novel will boost your marks. The whip is a symbol of tyranny and of Man. It is one of the instruments destroyed in Chapter 2, which causes the animals to 'caper with joy'. To see Napoleon carry one is a direct contradiction of the foundations of the Rebellion.

Before the other animals have a chance to vocalise their thoughts, as if on cue, the sheep begin to endlessly chant, 'Four legs good, two legs *better*!'

Clover asks Benjamin to read the writing on the barn wall where the Seven Commandments were originally inscribed, believing it to look different. When he does, he reads the one commandment that remains: 'All animals are equal but some animals are more equal than others.'

Pause for thought

After this, the supervising pigs carry whips and adopt much of human behaviour. What are some examples?

A week later, the pigs invite neighbouring farmers over to inspect Animal Farm. The farmers praise the pigs and express admiration for what they see. Later, the pigs and humans mingle in the farmhouse. The other animals, led by Clover, watch through a window as Pilkington and Napoleon toast each other. Pilkington states that the mistrust and misunderstandings of the past are over. He shows admiration for the way the pigs have managed to make Animal Farm's animals work harder and on less food than any other group of farm animals in the county and he says that he looks forward to introducing these advances on his own farm.

He declares that the farmers share a problem with the pigs: 'If you have your lower animals to contend with,' he says, 'we have our lower classes!' Napoleon responds by reassuring his human guests that the pigs never wanted anything other than to conduct business peacefully with their human neighbours, rather than 'stir up rebellion'. He explains that the pigs now own the farm and that animals on Animal Farm will no longer address one another as 'Comrade', or pay homage to old Major; nor will they salute a flag with a horn and hoof upon it. All of these customs have been changed recently by decree, he assures the men. Napoleon even announces that Animal Farm will now be known as Manor Farm, which is, he says, its 'correct and original name'.

The pigs and farmers return to their card game and the other animals creep away from the window. However, soon the sounds of a quarrel draw the animals back. Napoleon and Pilkington have both played the ace of spades; each accuses the other of cheating. As the animals watch through the window, they realise with horror that they can no longer distinguish between the pigs and the human beings: 'already it was impossible to say which was which.'

The gap in time between Chapter 9 and Chapter 10 allows Orwell to suggest the way in which the revolutionary ideals have disappeared. The old revolutionaries have become part of the machinery of the state and want to preserve things as they are, with the pigs in powerful administrative positions helped by the secret police (dogs). The meeting at the end of the novel between Pilkington, Frederick and Napoleon represents the conference held in Tehran in 1943 between Stalin (USSR), Roosevelt (USA) and Churchill (Britain). Orwell signals the Cold War with the quarrel at the end of the chapter. With his end sentence, Orwell suggests the lost hopes and ideals of the long-forgotten Rebellion.

Stalin, Roosevelt and Churchill at the 1943 conference in Tehran.

Pause for thought

Orwell said of the novel that it was 'primarily a satire on the Russian Revolution' but meant to be more far-reaching and to relate to any revolution that was 'violent and conspiratorial' and 'led by unconsciously power-hungry people'. He suggested that this sort of revolution could only result in a change of leaders. Consider how these intentions are evident in the novel.

Parallels between *Animal Farm* and Russian history

Animal Farm	**Russia**
Old Major's speech tells of an ideal world where all animals are treated fairly and equally	Marx, Engels and Lenin's thoughts on Marxism and socialism suggest a life of equality and freedom for Russian citizens
Animals suffer under human rule and Mr Jones; they revolt against him, seizing control of Manor Farm and forcing Mr Jones to leave	The workers (proletariat) suffer under the Romanov dynasty and Tsar Nicholas II; the working class seize control of Russia in the Bolshevik Revolution of February 1917, forcing Tsar Nicholas II to abdicate
The Battle of the Cowshed involves neighbouring farmers, who join with Mr Jones and attempt to regain control of Animal Farm, but Snowball leads the animals to victory and they remain in control	The counter-revolution involves the White Army, helped by Britain and France who did not want Communism to spread to Europe; they invade Russia but the Red Army, led by Trotsky, helps to keep the Bolsheviks in control
Snowball and Napoleon battle over power	Stalin and Trotsky seek control over Russia
Snowball is forcibly removed from the farm and the animals are told that he is an enemy	Stalin exiles Trotsky and tries to eliminate all traces of him, removing photographs of him
Napoleon claims Snowball's idea of the windmill as his own, after previously ridiculing it	Stalin starts the Five Year Plans, adopting Trotsky's previously rejected idea
Napoleon tells the hens to sell their eggs but they smash their eggs in protest	Stalin collectivises farms, placing them under state control, but the farm-owning peasants (kulaks) protest
Napoleon exaggerates the success of the farm with its new windmill when Whymper visits	Stalin exaggerates the success of his Five Year Plans
The animals suffer under Stalin's rule, with their rations being cut while the pigs are fed well	Stalin's economic policies lead to mass famine, with five million people starving to death between 1932 and 1934
Napoleon tightens his control over animals by brainwashing them into believing what he says and using propaganda to rewrite history; a picture of him is erected and a poem dedicated to him is written	Stalin's power increases and he tightens his grip over the Soviet Union through propaganda; he is said to be the wisest man in the world and pictures of him are erected in schools and factories
Napoleon starts his purges, eliminating anyone who expresses any dissent; four pigs who express unhappiness at the Sunday debate and the hens who led the egg rebellion are killed; Napoleon uses public confessions to create a climate of fear; even Boxer is killed	Stalin uses internal espionage to create a climate of fear with people informing on others thought to hold anti-Stalinist views; seven million people disappear between 1934 and 1938, some being given 'show trials' where they are forced to publicly confess their crimes; hardworking citizens are killed
Napoleon begins to sell timber to Frederick but is later tricked when Frederick pays with forged notes	The Soviet Union signs an anti-aggression pact with Germany but is later invaded by Germany in 1941
Frederick's men attack in the Battle of the Windmill; the animals win but suffer severe losses	The Germans attack the Soviet Union in the Battle of Stalingrad; they are defeated but the Soviet Union suffers heavy casualties
Pilkington visits Animal Farm	The Soviet Union and Britain sign a mutual aid agreement
The pigs and farmers have dinner together and play cards, but a quarrel breaks out over cheating	In 1943, Stalin attends the Tehran Conference where the Soviet Union, Britain and the USA claim to be allies, but a few years later the Cold War begins

Review your learning

(Answers available online)

1. Name the three main pigs on the farm.
2. With which historical event could the animals' rebellion be compared?
3. Which chapter is the first in which a commandment is altered?
4. Which animal dies in Chapter 9 and why is this important?
5. By the end of the novel, by what single commandment have all the commandments been replaced with?

More interactive questions and answers online.

Characterisation

- **How does Orwell reveal the characters to us?**
- **What evidence is there to help us think about each character?**
- **What is each character like?**
- **What role does each character play?**
- **What are the relationships between characters?**

Characters in a novel are revealed to us through a combination of techniques:

- direct description
- what characters say and how they say it
- what characters do
- what others say and think about them
- what they think themselves
- what they represent or symbolise

Orwell uses characters to explore political or moral stances, with Benjamin for example taking on the role of a disillusioned pessimist. They are seen to behave like humans, with their own behaviours and their own thoughts. In this way, they can be said to be anthropomorphic.

Old Major (Willingdon Beauty)

- is a prize Middle White Boar
- is wise
- is assertive
- is eloquent and persuasive
- is noble and revered
- is perceptive and wise
- represents Marx and Lenin

Orwell describes old Major as a 'majestic-looking pig' with a 'benevolent appearance', suggesting his status among the other animals as revered and respected. In his dream of rebellion, old Major shows himself to be an ambitious character whose vehemence about the commitment necessary for the rebellion indicates his assertiveness.

> ***Key quotation***
>
> **'And remember, comrades, your resolution must never falter.'**
>
> (Old Major, H5)

Old Major's speech in this chapter is a powerful piece of oration that inspires the animals to believe in a 'golden future time' when animals will be free. He speaks eloquently about his hopes for the future, persuading the animals into action.

Text focus

'And even the miserable lives we lead...until it is victorious.' (H4–5)
In this speech, Major rallies the animals to action, using a powerfully convincing speech. He uses a number of persuasive devices, including rhetorical questions, personal pronouns and emotive language. Words like 'miserable' and 'cruel' emphasise the sad plight of the animals, while his list of animals suggests that no one can escape this 'horror', as he calls it. He also uses alliteration in his rhetorical question when he asks, 'Is it not crystal clear then, comrades, that all the evils of this life of ours spring from the tyranny of human beings?' By describing humans as tyrants and using the possessive adjective 'ours', old Major depicts animals as victims united against Man. He also uses the device of contrast when he refers to 'night and day, body and soul', suggesting the way that animals must dedicate themselves to overthrowing humans. His use of exclamations, assertions and imperatives makes old Major's message clear — that the animals must 'pass on this message' of rebellion so that they are ultimately 'victorious'.

Old Major is optimistic in his hopes for the future and enthusiastic about the Rebellion and all it promises. It is evident that he is an intelligent and perceptive animal as he is able to assess the state of England at the time.

Key quotation

'No animal in England is free. The life of an animal is misery and slavery: that is the plain truth.'
(Old Major, H3)

He seeks to pass on his wisdom before he dies, telling the animals of his dream and teaching them the song 'Beasts of England'. He urges the animals to remember their duty of 'enmity towards Man and all his ways' (H6), and he can thus be seen to represent Karl Marx, Engels and Lenin.

Marx was a German philosopher interested in politics and economics who believed that capitalists exploited the workers/ proletariat in the same way that the humans are described as exploiting the animals in Orwell's novel. Marx worked with Friedrich Engels, another political thinker, to create the *Communist Manifesto* in 1848, in which he called for workers to unite against their chains and revolt against the capitalists, in the same way that old Major calls on the animals to rebel.

Vladimir Lenin was a great Communist revolutionary. He led the Bolshevik Revolution in 1917 and later became the first leader of the Soviet Union. Old Major's call for 'Rebellion' mirrors this.

Pause for thought

Look at how old Major is described in Chapter 1. How does Orwell suggest the esteem with which the other animals view him?

Napoleon

- is a leading pig
- is determined
- is fierce-looking and ruthless
- is tactical

- is power-hungry
- is Machiavellian
- is cruel
- is selfish and hypocritical
- represents Stalin

Napoleon investigates Farmer Jones's house, helping himself to food.

AF archive/Alamy

> **Pause for thought**
>
> Napoleon is described in Chapter 2 as 'fierce-looking' and as having a 'reputation for getting his own way' (H9). How does this suggest what is to come?

The name Napoleon is known all over the world because of the famous French leader Napoleon Bonaparte, who ruled France through tyranny in the nineteenth century. In the novel, Napoleon proves himself to be one of the leading pigs, and later the most dominant pig, on the farm. He is a power-hungry pig whose ruthlessness causes him to exile Snowball and use others to gain power.

Orwell uses Napoleon the character to represent Stalin, a ruthless dictator who ruled Russia with iron force. Just as Stalin did to the Russian people, Napoleon uses clever tactics to gain and maintain control over the animals. He uses food both as a reward and punishment — in Chapter 2 when the animals are rewarded after the Rebellion and in Chapter 6 when he uses the threat of half rations to force animals to work on a Sunday. He is contrasted with Snowball in his ability to canvass support from others and it is clear that he is tactical when he removes the dogs only for them to later appear as his trained assistants.

He is Machiavellian in his approach, using duplicity and cunning to maintain power. He increases the workload of the animals while decreasing their food rations, yet uses Squealer to suggest that this is not the case and insists that Sunday work is 'strictly voluntary'.

Napoleon's absence from the Battle of the Cowshed suggests his cowardice and when there are rumours about Snowball's plans to kill him, he sleeps with dogs guarding his bed and has a food taster.

Napoleon's ruthless desire to maintain power is seen when he starves the hens until they submit to his will and are forced to surrender their eggs, and when he slaughters animals in Chapter 7.

This, alongside the killing of Boxer — a much loved and hard-working member of the farm — and the subsequent acquirement of a crate of whisky from the proceeds of his sale, indicate the cruel and selfish nature of Napoleon.

His selfishness is seen early on when it is inferred that he drank the milk in Chapter 2, thus breaking the most important of the commandments (equality), almost immediately after the Rebellion. This selfishness increases as Napoleon starts to distance himself from the other animals, assuming emperor-like status and appearing only occasionally and then with dogs around him and announced by a cockerel. He has the poem written by Minimus inscribed on the barn wall and confers upon himself the 'Order of the Green Banner', all of which indicate both his selfishness and self-obsessed character.

Napoleon is hypocritical, breaking rules set for others. Despite forbidding the other pigs from eating sugar, he has it himself and he openly flouts the Seven Commandments, adopting the vices of humans and going against old Major's original tenets.

Like Stalin, whom he represents, Napoleon is an original revolutionary who betrays the ideals of the Rebellion, is corrupted by power and turns into a dictator.

Key quotation

'...there was a pile of corpses lying before Napoleon's feet and the air was heavy with the smell of blood, which had been unknown there since the expulsion of Jones.'

(H53)

Key quotation

'He took his meals alone, with two dogs to wait upon him, and always ate from the Crown Derby dinner service...'

(H57)

Snowball

- is creative and inventive
- is courageous
- is eloquent
- is intelligent
- is ambitious and tenacious
- is used as a scapegoat
- represents Trotsky

Snowball is a leading pig on the farm. Orwell uses him to represent Trotsky, who fought hard to ensure the success of the Russian Revolution. He believed in the ideals upon which the revolution was fought and sought to improve life for the Russian people. So, too, Snowball seeks to improve the ways in which the animals work.

In Chapter 2, he is described as 'vivacious' and 'inventive' and we see this side of his character in the novel in his enthusiastic and endless pursuit of improvements. We are told that he had studied the *Farmer and Stockbreeder* and 'was full of plans for innovations and improvements' (H30).

Key quotation

'Let us make it a point of honour to get in the harvest more quickly than Jones and his men could do.'

(Snowball, H15)

Like Trotsky, Snowball is an intelligent intellectual who organises the animals into committees and seeks to educate the illiterate masses. He is the one to explain to the animals the reason behind the flag's symbols of hoof and horn and he simplifies the Seven Commandments for the less intelligent animals to 'Four legs good, two legs bad'.

His intelligence and foresight are seen when, having studied books about the battle campaigns of Julius Caesar, he organises the animals for battle and leads them in an ambush on the humans in the Battle of the Cowshed. Here, too, we see his courage as he suffers a wound and is awarded 'Animal Hero, First Class'.

Key quotation

'Without halting for an instant Snowball flung his fifteen stone against Jones's legs.'

(H26)

He is the one to suggest and plan building a windmill to produce electricity and improve life for the animals. His tenacity is seen when despite Napoleon's contemptuous act of urinating on his plans he continues with them. It is in his speech about the windmill to the animals that we really see his eloquence first described in Chapter 2 (when we are told that 'he was quicker in speech' than Napoleon).

Key quotation

'By the time he had finished speaking, there was no doubt as to which way the vote would go.'

(H33)

As Trotsky was the natural successor to Lenin (Russia's first leader), Snowball is a natural leader able to inspire the animals with his ambitions for the farm and his eloquence. This is why he poses such a threat to Napoleon.

In 1927, Stalin exiled Trotsky and here, too, Napoleon has his dogs chase Snowball off the farm. Snowball becomes a scapegoat. He is slandered — said to have been 'in league with Jones from the very start' and later said to have 'never...received the order of "Animal Hero, First Class"' — and is blamed for anything that goes wrong on the farm.

Key quotation

'It seemed to them as though Snowball were some kind of invisible influence, pervading the air about them and menacing them will all kinds of dangers.'

(H49)

He becomes a tool used by Napoleon and the other pigs to create fear and maintain control over the other animals.

Squealer

- has a shrill voice but is a good talker
- is loyal to Napoleon
- is deceitful
- is dramatic
- is the voice of propaganda
- is threatening

Squealer is a key pig on the farm; he is used by Napoleon as the voice of propaganda. Where the pigeons initially spread the word of Animalism, Squealer spreads the word of the new regime under Napoleon.

Orwell uses him to show the way in which politicians manipulate language. Just as Joseph Stalin, through his role as general secretary in Russia, was able to control the press, Napoleon is able to control what information is provided and how it is delivered, through Squealer.

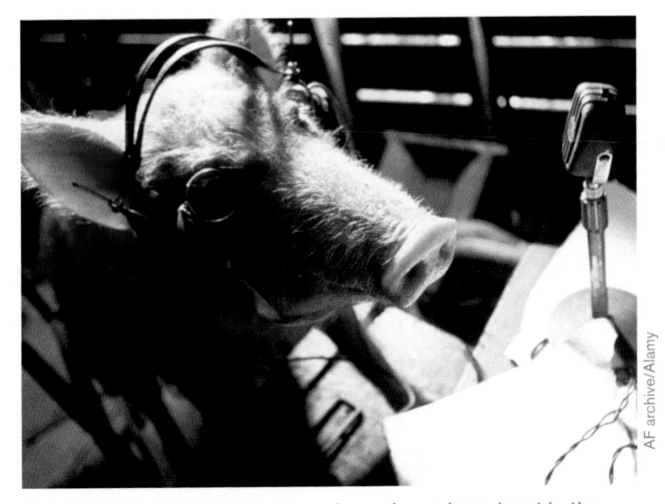

Squealer, the voice of propaganda, makes a broadcast in the 1999 film.

AF archive/Alamy

In Chapter 2, we are told that Squealer 'was a brilliant talker' and that he 'could turn black into white', suggesting his ability to persuade others. This skill is seen on numerous occasions as conditions on the farm deteriorate and as pigs assume more and more control.

We first see Squealer act as the voice of propaganda in Chapter 3 when he explains away the pigs eating the apples and milk because they are 'brain-workers' and need to protect the farm from Mr Jones (H22). Later he explains away Snowball's expulsion and rewrites history, stating that Napoleon was never really against the building of the windmill and that Snowball was Jones's secret agent all along. His silver-tongue and dramatic speeches help Napoleon justify his actions and policies by whatever means seem necessary.

Squealer uses a combination of strategies both simplifying and complicating language. By radically simplifying language and indoctrinating the sheep when he teaches them to bleat 'Four legs good, two legs *better*!', he limits the terms of debate and ensures the pigs' control. Similarly, by complicating language unnecessarily and using statistics and clever wording (such as his reference to 'tactics' in Chapter 5), he confuses and intimidates the uneducated animals. When he explains that the rations have been 'readjusted' not 'reduced', and when he tells the animals all that Napoleon does is for the good of the farm, he manipulates the animals into accepting what he says as truth.

Squealer's name fits him well in that it refers both to his 'shrill voice' which defines him and to his ability to betray his fellow animals. Squealer's deceitfulness is apparent in his actions: painting over the commandments as clearly seen in Chapter 8, claiming to have visited Boxer at his death bed and lying about old Major's tenets.

Squealer causes the animals to question their memories; using his persuasive skills and the fear of the dogs that attend him, he is always able to, as Orwell writes, 'put the matter in its proper perspective'.

Key quotation

'Are you certain that this is not something you have dreamed, comrades?'

(H41)

Text focus

'You have heard then, comrades...see Jones back?' (H42–H43)
In this speech, Squealer uses a number of rhetorical questions causing the animals to question their own memories and suspicions of the pigs. He uses personal pronouns such as 'you' repeatedly in an accusatory way, inferring that the animals are in the wrong to want the pigs not to have a proper rest or sleep in beds. He also refers to the animals as 'comrades' and uses the personal pronoun 'we' to suggest that he is on their side. His reference to the animals' absolute need for the pigs and their 'brainwork', along with his use of the emotive word 'surely', provokes guilt and instils a fear in the animals: that without the pigs, Jones would come back to rule the farm. By mentioning Jones, Squealer ensures that the animals' fear of a past master keeps their present one in control.

Key quotation

'Squealer spoke so persuasively, and the three dogs who happened to be with him growled so threateningly, that they accepted his explanation without further questions.'

(H37)

Key quotation

'Here Squealer's demeanour suddenly changed. He fell silent for a moment, and his little eyes darted suspicious glances from side to side before he proceeded.'

(H78)

Squealer also has a threatening presence; despite his apparent efforts to appease the animals, he is always attended by dogs who ensure that his message is accepted.

This more menacing side to Squealer is seen when Boxer questions his version of the Battle of the Cowshed in Chapter 7, only for Boxer to be attacked later in the chapter, and when Squealer informs the animals of the error they made in assuming Boxer was going to the knacker's yard in Chapter 9.

His defence of Napoleon's actions, describing his taking on the role of leader as a 'sacrifice' and indicating that everything that Napoleon does is for the benefit of all shows his loyalty to Napoleon. Squealer's lack of conscience is evident in the way in which he blatantly lies time and again. This and his unwavering loyalty to Napoleon make him the perfect propagandist for the tyrannical dictator Napoleon.

Boxer

- is hard-working
- is loyal
- is trusting
- is kind
- is strong
- is selfless
- represents the proletariat

Boxer is one of the cart-horses on the farm and as such he represents the working peasantry, or proletariat. He is described from the start as being 'as strong as any two horses put together'. After the Rebellion this strength increases, with Orwell stating that he 'seemed more like three horses than one' and describing him as having the strength equal to all the other animals put together.

This strength is put to great use both at harvest time and in the building of the windmill, where it is Boxer alone who is able to bring great boulders to a stop. He is integral to the success of farm.

His hard-working nature is epitomised in his personal motto of 'I will work harder' and the fact that he arranges with the cockerels to wake him earlier than the others.

Despite his physical strength, Boxer lacks intelligence and is therefore unable to learn his alphabet beyond the letter D, although he practises these letters religiously every day to remind himself of them.

His dedication to duty and commitment to the farm are evident in his hard work and consistent efforts, and it is this dedication and hard work that gain him the admiration of his fellow animals.

So when he collapses, it is natural for many of the animals to rush to the knoll to see what has happened. Boxer's selflessness is markedly apparent at this moment, when he thinks of the farm rather than of himself in saying that the others should be able to finish the windmill without him. His constant dedication to duty makes his cruel treatment at the hand of the pigs all the more callous.

Boxer's inability to see fault in the pigs contributes to his second motto of 'Napoleon is always right' and his belief that it must be some fault in the animals themselves that leads to the purges in Chapter 7.

However, it is this very loyalty and trusting nature that make him easy pickings for the pigs who exploit and abuse him, ultimately selling him to the knacker's yard and purchasing a crate of whisky with the proceeds.

Orwell uses Boxer as an example of the proletariat, and in particular a hard-working citizen who is exploited by the powers that be. Orwell may well have had Alexander Stakhanov in mind when creating Boxer. Stakhanov was a hard worker who was used by the Russian government as an example of productivity for other Soviet workers, in the same way that Napoleon, upon Boxer's death, suggests that the animals adopt as their own Boxer's two mottos.

However, despite appearing to wish to honour Boxer at the memorial banquet dedicated to him in Chapter 9, Napoleon and the other pigs insult his memory by drinking the whisky purchased from his sale to the knackers.

Key quotation

'Boxer with his tremendous muscles always pulled them through.'

(H17)

Key quotation

'...there were days when the entire work of the farm seemed to rest upon his mighty shoulders.'

(H17)

Key quotation

'Boxer was the admiration of everybody.'

(H17)

Benjamin

- is cynical and sceptical
- is intelligent
- is loyal to Boxer and Clover
- is the oldest animal on the farm
- could represent the moderate Russian
- could be a symbol of those who stand by and allow evil to prevail

Benjamin the donkey is described in Chapter 1 as 'the oldest animal on the farm and the worst tempered'. He is a cynic who does not believe that anything will change on the farm. He remains much the same as he always was after the Rebellion, 'never shirking and never volunteering for extra work either'.

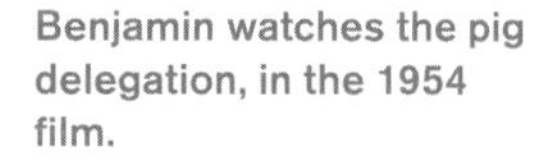

Benjamin watches the pig delegation, in the 1954 film.

AF archive/Alamy

His depiction as a donkey is quite significant in that he is not quite a horse (the proletariat) and yet definitely not a leader like the pigs, despite his intellect being equal to theirs.

Benjamin is a complex character. Some have suggested that he represents the older population of Russia, or that he represents the Menshevik intelligentsia — the intelligent section of the minority moderate Russian political party.

He refuses to express an opinion about the Rebellion and whether life will be better after it, offering instead cryptic responses. For the most part, Orwell uses him to represent those sceptics both in and out of Russia who believed that Communism would not help the Russian people, but who did not criticise it enough to lose their lives.

Benjamin's intelligence is apparent in that he 'could read as well as any pig' although he chooses not to exercise this skill. Later in Chapter 8, he is the only animal to fully comprehend what Snowball is doing with the paint, but again he chooses to say nothing. The only time he breaks this rule of saying nothing is when he reads what is written on the van that takes Boxer away. His loyalty to Boxer is described early on, and towards the end of the novel, when Boxer is unwell, Benjamin's commitment is evident in the way in which he sits with Boxer while he is ill.

Later in Chapter 10, when Clover asks Benjamin to read what is written on the barn wall, he does so but by this time it is too late — the pigs have well and truly taken over the farm and cannot be distinguished from the men with whom they are drinking.

Regardless of which sector of Russian society Benjamin represents, it could be argued that he is a symbol of intelligence that during the times of revolution and its aftermath is aware of what is going on but does nothing about it. His inaction may be explained away for he says, 'Donkeys live a long time.'

The name Benjamin means 'son of my right hand' or 'son of right'. This definition could support the argument made by many that Orwell intended Benjamin to be seen as a realist. Some people believe that Benjamin's cynicism reflects Orwell's own views of a Western world being eventually taken over by totalitarian governments. Certainly, Benjamin's views that nothing will ever be 'much better or much worse' but go on as it always has, turn out to be right in the world of the novel.

Key quotation

'...without openly admitting it, he was devoted to Boxer...'
(H2)

Pause for thought

Is it fair to describe Benjamin as apathetic? What do you think Orwell might have wished us to see as the reason or reasons behind Benjamin's lack of involvement in the Rebellion and its aftermath?

Mollie

- is vain
- is fickle
- is lazy and shirks work
- represents White Russians (middle class)
- represents those who defected to the West

Mollie is a 'pretty white mare' who pulls Jones's trap. She represents the White Russians who under tsarist rule had a privileged life, in her case represented by sugar and ribbons.

She is said to ask the 'stupidest questions' and is shown to have early reservations about life without Jones when she wants to keep her ribbons and sugar. Orwell states that she 'agreed but did not sound very convinced'. This is an indication of things to come when Mollie later defects to a neighbouring farm.

She is vain, looking at herself in the mirror in the farmhouse and learning only those letters that spell her name. Mollie is presented as a shirker who avoids work whenever possible.

At the Battle of the Cowshed, she is found hiding in her stall. This and her constant shirking of work present Mollie as a lazy and non-committed

member of the farm. Her desertion to a neighbouring farm represents those Russians who defected to the West in search of a better life.

Clover

- is kind and caring
- is motherly
- is loyal
- represents the proletariat
- is used to voice the thoughts of the animals

As a horse, Clover, like Boxer, represents the proletariat. She is depicted as a 'stout motherly mare' and her caring nature is seen early on in the novel when a brood of motherless ducklings files into the barn and she creates a wall behind which the ducklings nestle. We discover that she has lost four of her foals (they have been sold) and this may explain her motherly tendencies. Indeed, it is around her that the other animals huddle when several animals are killed in Chapter 7.

Clover is a constant whose kind and caring nature is seen throughout the novel and in particular in her loyalty to Boxer, whom she warns not to overstrain himself and whom she tends when he collapses.

We see that she has some intelligence as she is able to learn the whole alphabet, although she cannot read full words. It is this that allows her to recognise the change on the barn wall that Benjamin reads for her in Chapter 10.

Like Boxer, she is said never to lose heart, firmly believing in the ideals of the Rebellion. However, following the purges of Chapter 7, Orwell allows us a brief insight into her thoughts, as her 'eyes filled with tears'. He uses her to voice the thoughts of the other animals who, like her, lack the words to express themselves.

> ***Key quotation***
>
> **'If she could have spoken her thoughts, it would have been to say that this was not what they had aimed at when they had set themselves years ago to work for the overthrow of the human race.'**
>
> (H54)

Despite her disappointment about what is actually happening on the farm, she resolves to work hard and remain faithful, for there is 'no thought of rebellion or disobedience in her mind'. She decides to sing 'Beasts of England' as an expression of her belief in the ideals of Animalism, but even this is short-lived when Squealer bans the song, once again reinforcing her inability to express herself.

Clover, like Benjamin, is one of the few animals who live to the end of the novel. She remembers the Rebellion and the foundations upon which Animal Farm was built. This, then, explains the horror with which she greets the sight of Squealer on his hind legs.

She is a significant character for it is through her eyes that we intermittently see the ideals of Animalism eroding and it is she who leads the other animals to the window in the last chapter, when they witness the final destruction of all the principles upon which the Rebellion had been built.

The pigs

- represent the leadership
- are intelligent
- are greedy
- are corrupted by power

The pigs in the novel are depicted as the most intelligent of the animals. This is why, it is said in Chapter 2, they assume leadership.

However, Orwell signals for us the higher status that the pigs will assume later when they sit directly in front of the platform from which old Major delivers his speech in Chapter 1.

By Chapter 3, it is apparent that the pigs do not share in the animals' workload. Instead they 'directed and supervised the others' and when they start to give themselves bigger rations, taking the apple and milk, this is a solitary point on which both Napoleon and Snowball agree.

> ***Key quotation***
>
> **'The work of teaching and organizing the others fell naturally upon the pigs, who were generally recognized as being the cleverest of the animals.'**
>
> (H9)

> ***Key quotation***
>
> **'So it was agreed without further argument that the milk and the windfall apples (and also the main crop of apples when they ripened) should be reserved for the pigs alone.'**
>
> (H22)

Photos 12/Alamy

The pigs have become indistinguishable from Man (from the 1954 film).

Orwell uses the pigs to represent the revolutionaries corrupted by power, who enjoy their position at the top and seek to maintain the status quo, as a result. As the novel progresses, we see the way in which the pigs take on the role formerly occupied by Jones.

The dogs

- represent the secret police
- are loyal
- are trained

At the start of the novel, Orwell indicates the important role that the dogs will have when they are first to enter the barn to hear old Major's

speech. Their violence is also hinted at early on when they attack the rats in Chapter 1.

We are not fully aware of why Napoleon removes the dogs' puppies in Chapter 3 until they reappear to chase Snowball off the farm. However, thereafter, they play an important role in controlling the animals through fear, just as the secret police in Russia aided Stalin in his control over the masses.

Their loyalty to Napoleon is apparent in that they attend him wherever he goes and sit by his bedside while he sleeps. Orwell's description of their wagging tails when in Napoleon's presence draws a comparison between Napoleon and Jones. For this loyalty, the dogs are rewarded, enjoying a richer life than the other animals.

Key quotation

'Somehow it seemed as though the farm had grown richer without making the animals themselves any richer—except of course for the pigs and the dogs.'

(H81)

The sheep

- are unintelligent
- represent the general manipulated masses
- are used as tools to end debates

The sheep represent the most unintelligent sector of society. Snowball simplifies the commandments to the maxim of 'Four legs good, two legs bad' in order to help them understand Animalism, but they are easily manipulated by Napoleon who succeeds in canvassing their support. Their constant bleating of 'Four legs good, two legs bad!' interrupts meetings and suggests their lack of understanding. Later when they drown out Snowball's speech, we see the damage such blind support can cause: they unknowingly stifle free speech.

Later, they are easily manipulated by Squealer when he teaches them the mantra of 'Four legs good, two legs *better*'. Orwell uses them to represent those members of society who are used as tools for a cause and are manipulated for politicians' own ends.

Mr Jones

- is negligent
- is a hard master
- is a drunkard
- is cruel
- represents capitalism
- represents the aristocracy

Mr Jones is used by the writer to represent the aristocracy and ruling class in Russia, in particular Tsar Nicholas II who was shot along with all his family in the 1918 February Revolution. Mr Jones is portrayed as an uncaring man who neglects his animals and the farm, treating them cruelly and taking everything they produce. The opening sentence of the novel firmly establishes Mr Jones as a negligent figure, stating that he was 'too drunk' to tend to his duties properly.

The details provided by old Major in Chapter 1 suggest the tyranny with which Mr Jones rules the farm, his despicable attitude to the animals and the way in which he represents tsarism and capitalism. Indeed, the animals suffered under Jones's rule a similar fate to that of the peasants in Russia under tsarist rule.

> ***Key quotation***
>
> **'He sets them to work, he gives back to them the bare minimum that will prevent them from starving, and the rest he keeps for himself.'**
>
> (Old Major, H4)

Jones is described as always having been a 'hard master' but Orwell does not create a superficial image of him. Instead he points out that he had been a 'capable farmer' and had only taken to drink as a result of losing money in a lawsuit. Drink is his tonic and it is to this that he turns when the animals take over the farm. The sympathy he gains from his neighbouring farmers is false as Orwell indicates that they secretly wish to gain from his plight. In some ways we may feel sorry for Jones, but his cruelty indicated at the end of Chapter 1 when we are told that he fires 'the gun which always stood in a corner of his bedroom' prevents us from sympathising fully with him.

His attempts to regain the farm end in defeat and we are told in Chapter 10 that he has died 'in an inebriates' home in another part of the country'.

Jones does not physically feature much in the novel but he is constantly presented as the enemy. Throughout the novel, he is used by the pigs as a symbol of fear for the animals; his mere mention ensures the pigs' control.

Pilkington

- is a neighbouring farmer to Jones
- is a gentleman farmer
- represents Britain under Churchill
- is easy-going

Pilkington is one of Animal Farm's neighbouring farmers. His farm Foxwood is described as 'large, neglected' and 'old-fashioned'. Orwell describes him as a gentleman farmer who spends most of his time fishing or hunting.

Like Frederick, Pilkington fears the Rebellion extending to other farms and so he spreads rumours of wickedness on Animal Farm. Initially an enemy, Napoleon later befriends him.

Pilkington represents Britain under Churchill. His presence at the celebrations with Napoleon and Frederick at the end of the novel symbolises

Stalin and Churchill's alliance with Roosevelt at the Tehran Conference in 1943. The quarrel at the end indicates the Cold War that followed this time.

Frederick

- is a neighbouring farmer to Jones
- represents Germany under Hitler
- represents the USA under Roosevelt
- is tough and shrewd

Pilkington is another of Jones's neighbours. His farm Pinchfield is smaller but better kept than Frederick's, and Orwell describes him as 'a tough, shrewd man'. He is initially depicted as a man who drives a hard bargain and is said to be 'perpetually involved in lawsuits'.

This prepares us for the complicated negotiations over timber that he conducts with Napoleon. The way in which he tricks Napoleon with forged notes symbolises the way in which Russia was deceived by Germany under Hitler when, despite a non-aggression pact, Germany attacked Russia, causing much destruction.

In Chapter 10, Orwell uses Frederick to represent the USA under Roosevelt at the Tehran Conference, with the implied suggestion of the Cold War as a result of the quarrel at the end of the novel.

Moses

- is a raven
- shirks work
- is a tale-bearer
- represents organised religion
- tells tales of 'Sugarcandy Mountain'

Moses is depicted as Mr Jones's 'especial pet', a spy and tale-bearer. He represents organised religion, the state Church, placating the animals with tales of 'Sugarcandy Mountain', somewhere where animals go after a life of misery — in other words, a representation of Heaven. This reflects Marx's view that religion was an 'opiate of the masses' that promised a wonderful afterlife in an effort to anaesthetise people from the pain of their real lives and in doing so, according to him, religion prevented people from changing their lives for the better.

Moses is a useful ally to Jones and the pigs as he promises the animals that all their hardships will be rewarded in 'Sugarcandy Mountain'. By presenting Moses in this way, it is as if Orwell is suggesting that organised religion supports the power of the state and not the ordinary man.

Character	Who/what s/he represents
Jones	Capitalism/aristocracy
Mollie	White Russians (middle classes)
Boxer/ Clover	Workers/proletariat
Benjamin	Cynic/aging population/Menshevik intelligentsia
Dogs	Secret police
Major	Marx/Lenin/Engels
Napoleon	Stalin
Snowball	Trotsky
Squealer	Information officer/propaganda/media
Pigs	Officials of the Communist Party
Moses	Organised religion
Pilkington	Britain under Churchill
Frederick	Germany under Hitler/the USA under Roosevelt

Grade *focus*

Character questions are commonplace. Look at the *Sample essays* section to see what sorts of questions you could face on character. Being able to write with confidence about characters and make insightful comments rather than just simple ones will get you the better grade. Knowing what or who characters represent and how their language reflects this is a sign of a higher-level candidate. For example, writing that Squealer is used by Orwell to represent the media and propaganda hence his constant references to Jones and his manipulation of language devices used to control the animals, is better than writing that Squealer is a good talker who has a shrill voice

Review your learning

(Answers available online)

1. In what different ways can characters be revealed to us by a writer?
2. Write down three adjectives to describe Napoleon and three to describe Snowball.
3. Which animals represent the most stupid sector of society?
4. Which character represents organised religion?
5. List the characters who represent the following: Marx, Stalin, Trotsky, the Menshevik intelligentsia, those who defected to the West and the secret police.

More interactive questions and answers online.

Themes

- **What is a theme?**
- **What are the main themes in *Animal Farm*?**
- **How do these themes relate to each other?**
- **How do these themes relate to characters?**

A theme in a text is a key idea that the writer explores. There is no definitive way to identify the themes in any one text and there will be overlaps between themes. However, you can think about key events and characters, the impression left with you at the end of the novel and any repeated imagery to help you determine some of the themes in *Animal Farm*. Here are key ideas/themes that Orwell explores in his novel:

- power
- hierarchy
- violence and power
- knowledge and power
- language and power
- resources and power
- cruelty and abuse of power
- lies and deception
- ideals: utopia
- reality: dystopia
- history and collective memory

Power

A key theme in the novel is power and the way in which it is used to manipulate others and to maintain control over the masses. In the *Style* section, you will read about how the novel is a satire. It is a satire on political power and the corrupting influence of power. Lord Acton famously said, 'power corrupts and absolute power corrupts absolutely'. It is this very idea that Orwell explores in *Animal Farm*. Having fought in the Spanish Civil War, Orwell had come to the conclusion that there was something in human nature that will always seek violence, conflict and power over others. He uses *Animal Farm* to demonstrate this.

Hierarchy

From the start of the novel, we are aware of existing power structures among the animals. Orwell makes this clear in the way in which the animals are described. It is evident that old Major is a respected animal and, as a prize-winning boar, he has physical prowess over other animals. The same could be said for Napoleon, who is described as 'fierce-looking' and whom Jones is breeding for sale, suggesting his superior physical attributes. Aside from this, it is evident that the pigs and dogs enjoy a higher status than the other animals as they sit directly in front of the platform upon which old Major is ensconced in Chapter 1. By Chapter 2, we are told explicitly that the pigs are 'generally recognized as being the cleverest of the animals', so Orwell sets the stage for their assumption of power.

Violence and power

The violent side of power is evident in the first chapter when Jones is described by old Major and we see the way in which he is able to instil fear in the animals. When we are told that Jones's gun 'always stood in the corner of his bedroom', we realise how violence and fear are part of the tools of control and power for Jones and his men. It quickly becomes obvious that this is also the case for the pigs, who use the dogs to ensure that the animals cooperate, in the same way that the Communists in Russia used the secret police.

The dogs' propensity for violence is seen as early as Chapter 1 when they suddenly catch sight of the rats and make a dash for them. Napoleon's recognition of the way in which violence will aid him is evident when in Chapter 3 he removes Jessie and Bluebell's nine puppies, making himself 'responsible for their education', only for them to reappear fully trained in Chapter 5 when they are described as 'enormous'. The impact that the dogs have on the other animals is apparent as the latter are described as 'silent and terrified'. From this point onwards, both Squealer and Napoleon use the dogs to ensure they maintain control over the animals.

Napoleon removes the puppies to train them as his secret police.

Pause for thought

Closely linked with violence is the theme of fear. Consider how we see this in the novel.

The final aspect of violence appears in Chapter 10 when we see Napoleon and the other pigs carry whips — another way in which they are using violence to control the animals. When in Chapter 2 the animals burn the tools used by humans, they are presented as freeing themselves from human control. Therefore, the pigs' carrying whips signifies a complete turnabout. The pigs have now taken on all the aspects of human beings that they despised at the beginning of the novel.

Knowledge and power

Pause for thought

Read the analysis of Benjamin's character earlier in this guide. Consider why you think Orwell depicted him as a cynic.

The pigs' superior intelligence and ability to read allows them to lead the animals and exert power over them. This is evident when we are told that the 'stupider animals such as the sheep, hens and ducks were unable to learn the Seven Commandments by heart' and so Snowball simplified these into the maxim of 'Four legs good, two legs bad'. Orwell constantly draws our attention to the difference in intelligence between animals and he uses this to explain the blind commitment that some animals show to the farm and their acceptance of all that the pigs do.

The only animal whose intelligence equals that of the pigs is Benjamin, but Orwell depicts him as a cynic unwilling to involve himself in events.

Key quotation

'On Sunday mornings Squealer, holding down a long strip of paper with his trotter, would read out to them lists of figures proving that the production of every class of foodstuff had increased by 200 per cent, 300 per cent, or 500 per cent, as the case might be.'

(H57)

The fact that the pigs are described as 'brain-workers' allows them to maintain power over the other animals who are told they may make the wrong decision and then Jones would come back. The pigs' superior knowledge is used to maintain control. Through Squealer's references to statistics, Orwell shows the way in which those in power on the farm use knowledge and, in this case, fictitious numbers to maintain control over the animals.

Language and power

Key quotation

'The birds did not understand Snowball's long words but they accepted his explanation...'

(H21)

Closely related to the idea of knowledge and power is language and power. There are numerous examples in the text of the way in which language is used to maintain power. As early as Chapter 3, we see Snowball's superior linguistic ability when he uses the words 'propulsion' and 'manipulation', which the birds do not understand.

Later we see Squealer using language as a device to maintain the pigs' power, when he talks of 'tactics' in Chapter 5, which the animals do not understand and when we are told that he refers to 'mysterious things' called 'files', 'reports' and 'memoranda', with the implied suggestion that these are unintelligible to the animals.

The animals' inability to express their thoughts aloud, which we are told of by the narrator on numerous occasions, demonstrates their linguistic weaknesses, which in turn limit their power. It is this that Orwell wishes to highlight.

In his essay *Literature and Totalitarianism*, Orwell wrote that totalitarianism 'abolished freedom of thought' by telling people what to think. The reduction of the Seven Commandments to one maxim is an example of the way in which the animals' thoughts are limited.

When Napoleon gets the sheep on his side and they bleat continuously in meetings, we see the way in which their blindness erodes freedom of speech also. In the last chapter, this is made apparent when Orwell writes that the animals, despite their lack of power over language, 'might have uttered some word of protest. But just at that moment, as though at a signal, all the sheep burst out into a tremendous bleating of — 'Four legs good, two legs *better*!...' (H84)

Squealer's ability to manipulate language is apparent from the start when he is described as being able to change 'black into white' and we see in his speeches the way in which he uses persuasive devices to good effect. His rhetorical questions, lists, choices of inclusion and omission and personal pronouns are all tools that help to pacify the animals and maintain the pigs' power (for a 'Text focus' box on Squealer's oratory skills, see page 42).

Key quotation

'Even Boxer was vaguely troubled. He...tried hard to marshal his thoughts; but in the end he could not think of anything to say.'

(H34)

Resources and power

Another device that the pigs use to maintain power is their access to resources. Napoleon uses food to maintain control over the animals. He uses it as a reward in Chapter 2 and as a punishment in Chapter 6.

Money is also a resource that allows the pigs to have power, for it is this money that enables them to buy the necessary goods (oil, nails, string, dog biscuits) for the farm and whisky for themselves. When Napoleon sells the timber to Frederick, the animals are made to file past the money, which is presented on a china dish like food.

Later, we see Napoleon state that he wants 'normal business relations with their neighbours' indicating the importance he places on trade as he recognises the power this gives him.

Cruelty and abuse of power

Mr Jones and his men's violent reaction to the animals suggests the lack of understanding that the humans have for the animals in the same way that the aristocracy of Russia did not understand what it was like to be poor. Just as in Russia the maltreatment of the poor provokes a rebellion, on the farm Jones's maltreatment of the animals leads to rebellion.

The list of items used in 'Jones's hated reign' helps to convey to readers the cruel treatment of the animals. Orwell itemises the 'bits', 'the nose rings', 'the dog chains', 'the cruel knives' and more and has the animals ritualistically burn these reminders of their torture, describing them as 'caper[ing] with joy' when they see the whips — as symbol of their maltreatment — 'going up in flames'.

Later, when several animals are killed in Chapter 7, Orwell shows the way in which the new regime has been corrupted by power and has turned to the cruel tactics of their predecessors. When Boxer is killed for a crate of whisky, we again see the brutal tendencies of the pigs and, if the constant references to the reduced rations and hard work of the animals were not enough, when the pigs start to carry whips, Orwell makes clear for us the way in which the pigs have fully adopted a cruel attitude towards their fellow animals.

Lies and deception

Pause for thought

The animals trust the leadership despite not fully understanding events. Think of incidents when this trust is shown to be misplaced because the animals are deceived.

The novel is full of examples of deception being used as a tool to both maintain control over the animals and protect the farm against neighbouring farms. Squealer lies about the commandments and changes to ideals, about Snowball, about history and about farm production to the animals to delude them into thinking they are well off.

Napoleon and (unwittingly) the other animals conspire in deceiving the humans into believing food is plentiful on Animal Farm when Napoleon shows Whymper around the farm in Chapter 7.

In Chapter 10, Orwell shows the extent of the lies and deception on the farm when Napoleon betrays all the ideals of the Rebellion — when the pigs are said to now own the farm, the term 'comrades' is to be dropped and the name Manor Farm is to be reinstated. Orwell's experience had led him to believe as he once said that, 'In a time of universal deceit, telling the truth is a revolutionary act.'

Ideals: utopia

Orwell said that *Animal Farm* was founded on the basis of a utopian world — an ideal that old Major describes in his speech at the start of the novel and to which the narrator refers back throughout the text. The utopian world that is depicted is encapsulated in the song 'Beasts of England'. This serves as a national anthem for the animals' cause and reminds us of 'The red flag', a famous socialist song written by James Connell in 1889, and of the 'Internationale', the international communist anthem written in 1871 by Eugène Pottier. In 'Beasts of England', Orwell presents us with many positive words such as 'joyful tidings', 'golden future time', 'fruitful fields' and 'riches more than mind can picture', along with references to freedom. All of these words convey the idyllic image of a happy future full of prosperity and freedom to which the animals look forward.

This ideal appears to become a reality in Chapter 2, straight after the Rebellion.

Text focus

'But they woke at dawn...now they could hardly believe that it was all their own.' (H13)

The symbolism of the animals waking at dawn is clear as it suggests a new beginning for them — a rebirth. This is emphasised when Orwell later writes 'It was as though they had never seen these things before'. Words such as 'glorious' and 'clear morning light' indicate the purity of the utopian world that has come about as a result of the Rebellion. The repetition of the word 'theirs' suggests the importance of ownership and conveys the Socialist ideals of freedom and collectivism. Orwell communicates the animals' absolute joy through words such as 'ecstasy', 'gambolled' and 'leaps of excitement', thus conveying the euphoria associated with freedom and ownership, which are again referred to when he repeats 'they could hardly believe that it was all their own'.

The placement of the speech at the start of the novel ensures that readers are aware of the utopian world to which the animals aspire. By referring back to old Major's speech throughout the novel, Orwell uses the speech as a benchmark against which we can judge events. This ensures that we are aware of the way in which this ideal is being corrupted.

Orwell makes evident the way in which the animals at first enjoy this ideal when he writes that 'Every mouthful of food was an acute positive pleasure, now that it was truly their own food, produced by themselves and for themselves' (H17). By the end of the novel, despite the gradual deterioration in conditions and the obvious breaking of commandments, the animals hold on to this ideal, believing in it.

Orwell shows the way in which the masses are deluded into believing in an ideal, only to be exploited by those in power as this ideal is corrupted.

Key quotation

'And yet the animals never gave up hope... They were still the only farm in the whole country—in all England!—owned and operated by animals.'

(H82)

Reality: dystopia

Orwell shows that the way in which the ideal vision that old Major presents in Chapter 1 is altered is the same way that the socialist ideal that he saw in Spain was lost. First evidence of this is seen in Chapter 2 when the pigs are identified as most clever, thus differentiating between the

Grade **booster**

Knowing how Orwell's experiences in the Spanish Civil War affected him will help you to explain why Orwell presents the events that occur in *Animal Farm* in this way.

animals and going against the tenet of equality. When Napoleon remains behind with the milk only for it to disappear, we can see what the animals cannot, and we are therefore unsurprised to read of the pigs directing the others to work in Chapter 3. In Chapter 5, the animals are described as having 'worked like slaves' and their food is described as no less than in Jones's time, so it is clear that the world is less of an ideal now for the animals than in Chapter 2, although Orwell ironically points out that 'they grudged no effort or sacrifice' because what they were doing was for 'the benefit of themselves...and not for a pack of idle thieving human beings'. He makes clear that the animals still believe in the ideal. However, when Napoleon announces he will engage in trade, Orwell draws our attention back to old Major's speech and refers to the animals' 'vague uneasiness'.

Key quotation

'These scenes of terror and slaughter were not what they had looked forward to on that night when old Major first stirred them to rebellion.'

(H54)

When animals are killed in Chapter 7, Orwell allows Clover's thoughts to be seen and in them he contrasts the dystopian reality with the utopian ideals of the Rebellion.

The dystopian world is described clearly for us through Clover's unspoken thoughts.

***Text* focus**

'Instead she did not know why they had come...confessing to shocking crimes.' (H55)

Orwell uses a list to convey the horror of the dystopian world that the animals now endure: lack of free speech, terror and murder. He uses emotive language to emphasise the sadness of the situation with words such as 'fierce', 'growling' and 'shocking', conveying the absolute fear faced by the animals. The lack of freedom in this dystopian world is emphasised through the words 'had to', and the inclusion of the words 'comrades' is an ironic reminder of the utopian ideals of the Rebellion.

Key quotation

'Sometimes the older ones among them racked their dim memories and tried to determine whether in the early days of the Rebellion, when Jones's expulsion was still recent, things had been better or worse than now. They could not remember.'

(H81–82)

By Chapter 10, Napoleon's hold over the animals is definite. Many of the commandments have been broken and the pigs and dogs enjoy a comfortable life while the other animals suffer. Orwell presents a dystopian world where the ideals of Chapters 1 and 2 have been corrupted but no one, except Benjamin who refuses to talk, can remember.

History and collective memory

The novel shows the way in which history is rewritten by the pigs, with very few animals surviving at the end to recall distant events. The barn wall serves as a symbol of collective memory that is gradually changed and eroded by the pigs. Orwell makes clear the way in which Squealer gets the animals to question and doubt their memories so that they end up forgetting the past.

We literally see him turning 'black into white' as he manipulates the animals into believing the rewritten history: 'Do you not remember how, just at the moment when Jones and his men had got inside the yard, Snowball suddenly turned and fled, and many animals followed him?' (H51)

By doing this, Orwell shows the way in which the past and future are controlled by those who hold power in the present. As he said in his novel *Nineteen Eighty-Four*, 'Who controls the past controls the future; who controls the present controls the past.'

Key quotation

'...the animals were satisfied that they had been mistaken.' (H41)

Grade ***focus***

Theme questions are commonplace. Look at the *Sample essays* section to see what sorts of questions you could face on themes. Being able to write with confidence about themes and make insightful comments rather than just simple ones will get you the better grade. Exploring how the theme of memory is developed through the character of Squealer and his role as information officer will get you a better grade than simply stating how some animals' memories are good or bad.

Review your learning

(Answers available online)

1. What is a theme?
2. Make a list of themes that appear in the novel and that you have learned about in this section. Add any more you can think of.
3. How is the barn used as a symbol?
4. Which animals contribute to the erosion of free speech?
5. Give three examples of lies.

More interactive questions and answers online.

Style

- **What does 'style' mean?**
- **What type of novel is *Animal Farm*?**
- **What narrative voice is employed?**
- **What sort of language is used in the novel?**

The style of a text refers to the way in which it is written. How Orwell wrote the novel and the choices he made in terms of overall structure, narrative voice, language and imagery are important for you to understand his intentions and the craft of the novel. They will help you to write more convincingly about the book.

The areas you will focus on to help you understand the style of *Animal Farm* are:

- satire
- allegory
- symbolism
- fairy tales
- animal stories
- narrative voice
- point of view
- dialogue
- structure
- language and imagery
- repetition
- tone and irony
- propaganda: the power of language
- imagery
- comedy

Satire

A satire is a text that comments on a system or structure in society, often poking fun at or ridiculing it. The critic V.C. Pritchett once called Orwell 'the wintry conscience of a generation'. His works suggest that he saw himself as the exposer of painful truths and as a representative of the English moral conscience. In his preface to the original edition of *Animal Farm*, Orwell stated that he was criticising Stalin's regime in the Soviet Union. It is clear that in writing *Animal Farm* Orwell makes comments on power structures in human society and the hypocrisy and loss of ideals in the Communist regime following the Russian Revolution. As such, the novel can be seen as a satire on society and on Russian history in particular.

In reducing well-known political and historical figures to animals, Orwell ridicules them. The whole notion of comparing bureaucrats and leaders to pigs is comic, given the associations we have of pigs being greedy and dirty. Aptly, the pigs on *Animal Farm* prove themselves to be both greedy for food and for power and dirty in the sense that they are corrupt.

The sheeps' chant of 'Four legs good, two legs bad!' pokes fun at the political chants that certain sectors of society adopt without necessarily understanding what they mean. Similarly, Orwell ridicules systems of government, for example in Chapter 10 when the pigs explain to the animals that they are involved in very important work related to 'reports' and administrative tasks. Minimus's poem about Napoleon is also full of humour; it is a dig at the trite eulogies that dictators and in particular the Communist regime used as propaganda.

It is therefore accurate to describe the style of *Animal Farm* as satirical. In fact, Orwell wrote other satirical novels, such as *Nineteen Eighty-Four* in which he depicted a futuristic world where the government has excessive power over citizens.

Pause for thought

Other examples of satirical texts are *Gulliver's Travels* by Jonathan Swift and *Brave New World* by Aldous Huxley. See if you can find out what these novels satirise.

Allegory

An allegory is a story or fable that represents something else. *Animal Farm* is an allegory of Russian history and in particular the Russian Revolution and the Communist regime that followed it. Events in the novel correspond with those during the early twentieth century in Russia and characters in the book represent historical figures such as Tsar Nicholas II, Marx, Trotsky and Stalin. For a more detailed breakdown of the way in which events relate to history and characters, look at the chapters on *Plot and structure* and *Characterisation*.

Symbolism

Part of any allegorical text is symbolism — the way in which events, characters and motifs represent other things. Orwell uses the sheep, horses and in particular Boxer to symbolise the proletariat — the working classes — and Mr Jones to symbolise the aristocracy — the tsarist rulers. He uses the animals' flag to symbolise the Red Banner of the Russian Communist era and so on. Detailed below is a brief breakdown of symbols, other than those relating to characters and plot.

Pause for thought

Can you think of any other symbols in the novel?

Symbol	What it represents
Animal Farm	Communist Russia/society in general
The barn	Collective human memory/history
Dog chains	Oppression
Whip	Tyranny
Hoof and horn	Animal freedom, equivalent to the Red Banner
Ribbons and sugar	Slavery to man (Chapter 2)/privilege (Chapter 9)
Minimus's poem about Napoleon	Propaganda
Money	Power
Windmill	Industry

Fairy tales

Pause for thought

When Orwell sought to publish his novel, one publisher rejected the novel because he felt there was no market for children's books.
Do you think *Animal Farm* is a children's book?

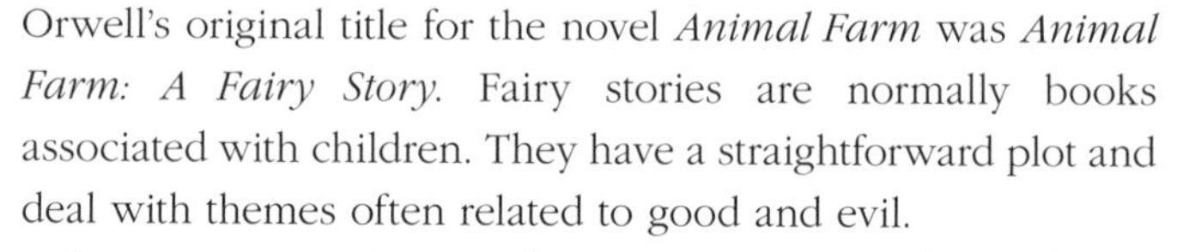

Orwell's original title for the novel *Animal Farm* was *Animal Farm: A Fairy Story*. Fairy stories are normally books associated with children. They have a straightforward plot and deal with themes often related to good and evil.

In some ways the novel can be seen as a fairy tale. Its setting of a farm and the animal characters suggest that the book is suitable for children. Also the novel deals with good and evil in the same way that many fairy tales like *Hansel and Gretel* and *Little Red Riding Hood* do. However, in *Animal Farm*, unlike in most fairy tales, good is not rewarded; it does not triumph. Evil is seen to prevail. Where many fairy tales present us with an idyllic or utopian world, *Animal Farm* shows the movement from utopia to dystopia. *Animal Farm* is not really a fairy story in the traditional sense but rather a political satire.

It is therefore understandable that many publishers dropped the subtitle '*A Fairy Story*' and often in translation the words *A Satire*, *A Contemporary Satire* or *Adventure* or *Tale* were used.

Grade **booster**

Knowing that a utopian world is one based on ideals and a dystopian world — its opposite — is one where terror and deprivation reign, will help you to describe the change in the novel and gain you extra marks.

Animal stories

There is a long tradition of presenting animals in children's books. With its subtitle of '*A Fairy Story*', its farm setting and use of animal characters, some may argue that *Animal Farm* is a perfect children's book. Without knowing the political background to the text, someone might read the novel on a simple level as a story about animals. However, even the simplest animal stories often carry a moral.

The most famous examples are Aesop's fables. Here animals are used as characters in a range of tales each carrying a moral. The *Tortoise and the Hare*, for example, teaches children about the benefits of patience for 'slow and steady wins the race'. Many of Orwell's literary studies and writings focus on economic and social injustice. In an essay called 'Why I Write' (1947), Orwell wrote of his desire 'to make political writing into an art'. He wrote from 'a sense of injustice', not from the idea that he was going to produce a great work of art: 'I write it because there is some lie I want to expose, some fact to which I want to draw attention, and my initial concern is to get a hearing.'

Ivy Close Images/Alamy

Aesop's fable *The Tortoise and the Hare* teaches the benefits of patience.

In this way, Orwell's use of animals in *Animal Farm* can be seen as a deliberate device. By using animals, he was able to draw on the traditions of moral animal stories and deliver a lesson to his readers.

There are many benefits to animal stories: they can make life seem simple and straightforward, thus making Orwell's message about the dangers of power clearer and more direct. The use of animals helps readers to more easily distinguish between characters and in this case to make associations. We come to see the horses as workers, the pigs as leaders and the sheep as stupid. In some ways, animals are easier to laugh at than humans, and as Orwell was satirising events and people, his use of animals helps him in his purpose. Finally, by using animals, writers are able to create a fantasy world where anything can happen. We are, therefore, unsurprised when a pig is seen wearing a hat or walking on his hind legs because Orwell has created a fantasy world for us, and as with all good fantasy its roots lie in reality.

Pause for thought

Make a list of stories you know which involve animal characters. Can you figure out what their morals/lessons are?

Narrative voice

Narrative voice is the voice of the person telling the story. It controls how the story is communicated to the audience. In *Animal Farm*, Orwell employs the third-person omniscient voice. In other words, the story is narrated by an outsider who has insight into all characters' thoughts and feelings. This creates distance for the reader in that we view events from the outside, but it also allows us intermittent insight into characters, helping us to understand their motivations and reactions to events. Sometimes Orwell allows us insight into the animals' reactions as a whole, such as when we are told how they feel about the windmill.

Key quotation

'The whole farm was deeply divided on the subject of the windmill.'

(H31)

> ***Key quotation***
>
> **'A few animals still felt faintly doubtful...'** (H40–41)
>
> **'Napoleon was well aware of the bad results that might follow if the real facts of the food situation were known...'** (H46)
>
> **'If she herself had had any picture of the future, it had been of a society of animals set free from hunger and the whip, all equal...'** (H54)

> ***Key quotation***
>
> **'Yes it was theirs—everything that they could see was theirs!'** (H13)
>
> **'The creatures outside looked from pig to man, and from man to pig, and from pig to man again; but already it was impossible to say which was which.'** (H89)

> ***Key quotation***
>
> **'"Does it not say something about sleeping in a bed?"**
>
> **...Curiously enough, Clover had not remembered that the Fourth Commandment mentioned sheets; but as it was there on the wall, it must have done so.'** (H42)

> ***Key quotation***
>
> **'Bravery is not enough,' said Squealer. 'Loyalty and obedience are more important.'** (H35)

> **Pause for thought**
>
> Look through the novel at the references to time. Make a list of five so that you can see the simple way in which the story moves forward.

And sometimes he pinpoints individual characters/ groups of characters whose thoughts we are made privy to.

Point of view

Point of view or viewpoint refers to the perspective from which the story is viewed. The novel is told by an external narrator but we see events mostly through the eyes of the common animals on the farm. It is through their eyes that we see the Rebellion occur and at the end of the novel, it is through their eyes that we see the pigs and men.

Dialogue

By using an omniscient narrator, Orwell allows us direct access to the animals' thoughts, but he supplements this with dialogue between animals. It is through this dialogue that he moves the plot forward, giving us greater insight into characters and their reactions. For example, when Clover asks Muriel to read the Fourth Commandment in Chapter 6, Orwell later uses the narrative voice to describe her feelings and response to what she reads.

Orwell also uses dialogue to convey the animals' political or ideological theories. In particular we see the way in which Squealer uses what he says to manipulate others and to deliver Napoleon's political intentions.

Structure

With his use of an external narrator, Orwell provides us with a traditional storyteller who unfolds the story for us. He opens the story with a focus on character and setting before moving on to events which, as we have seen, relate to history. The narrator signals time passing and events for us in a simplified way: 'Three nights later old Major died peacefully in his sleep' (H8); 'All through that summer' (H17); 'By the late summer' (H22).

Animal Farm is a novella — a short novel — and while the plot is heavily linked with historical events, Orwell still loosely follows traditions of structure in that he provides us with an exposition, complication, rising, action, climax, falling action and resolution.

If we were to view the movement of the novel as a graph, we might see it as follows:

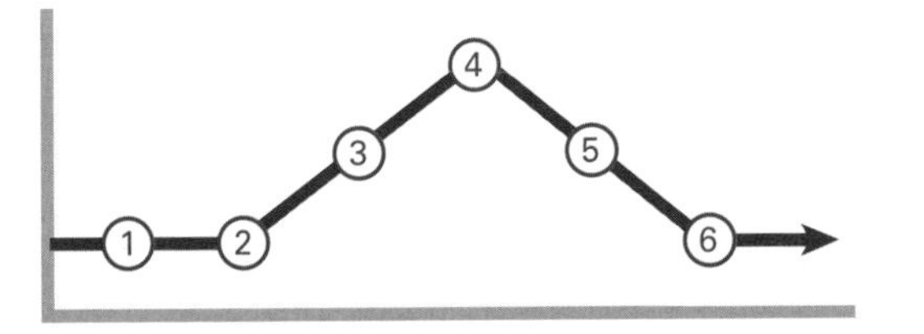

① Exposition — introduction to characters, background, context and themes
② Complication/inciting moment — a problem is introduced
③ Rising action — the plot thickens: more complications and obstacles are presented
④ Climax — the peak moment in the play
⑤ Falling action — things begin to settle
⑥ Resolution/denouement — loose ends are tied up

Pause for thought

In a letter that Orwell wrote to Dwight Macdonald, editor of the American journal *Politics*, he said that he wanted the moral in *Animal Farm* to be 'that revolutions only effect a radical improvement when the masses are alert and know how to chuck out their leaders as soon as the latter have done their job.' He said that 'The turning point of the story was supposed to be when the pigs kept the milk and apples for themselves'. Do you think that this is the turning point in the novel? Why?

Language and imagery

The actual language that Orwell uses is direct and for the most part simple. It appears to be colloquial and what one might expect in a fairy tale although it is deceptive, for, as you have seen, *Animal Farm* is much more than a fairy tale.

Orwell writes simply and concisely, using few words but choosing them carefully. His use of multiple adjectives and of lists helps him to convey much information and descriptive detail for readers in a short space of time. For example, in the space of four words, he is able to give us a lot of information about Mollie when he describes her as a 'foolish, pretty white mare'.

In addition to this, Orwell employs some of the traditional language devices we might see in a fairy tale.

Repetition

Just as in fairy tales where events and key phrases are repeated, Orwell uses repetition in *Animal Farm*. The changes made to commandments and the frequent references to the animals' bad memories are repeated patterns in the novel in the same way that Goldilocks's attempts at eating three different bowls of porridge, sitting on three different chairs and sleeping in three different beds are repeated patterns in the fairy tale of *Goldilocks and the Three Bears*.

Alongside repeated events, Orwell uses repetition of language. An obvious example is the bleating of the sheep with their chant of 'Four legs good, two legs bad!' This reflects the blind political fervour that Orwell is criticising. Other phrases such as 'Napoleon is always right' and 'I will work harder' reflect the mottos that individuals adopt in life and the sorts of catch phrases we often see in fairy tales — 'I'll huff and I'll puff and I'll blow your house down', for example. Orwell also uses repetition of words or phrases such as 'comrades' when referring to the original ideals of Animalism. Other repeated words include 'victory', 'triumph' and increasingly 'death' as the novel progresses. The animals are also described as working 'like slaves' on a couple of occasions, with the word 'worked' occurring a number of times. In this way, Orwell is able to suggest the worsening conditions on the farm and the hard work the animals endure.

Pause for thought

Why do you think the words 'triumph' and 'victory' occur frequently in the novel?

Tone and irony

The tone of a text refers to the manner in which an author expresses his or her attitude or ideas. In *Animal Farm*, Orwell uses his omniscient narrator to convey his own opinion about historical events. The tone he uses is one of detachment and distance — events are presented in a very matter-of-fact way.

However, despite this apparent detachment, Orwell manages to create a distinct sense of irony through choice wording and devices such as exaggeration and understatement. For example, when he writes in Chapter 7, 'It was about this time that the pigs suddenly moved into the farmhouse and took up their residence there' (H42), he creates irony. The opening of the sentence ('It was about this time') makes the event sound commonplace. In this way, Orwell understates the event and its consequences. It is as if what he is writing about were an everyday occurrence, using a distant, detached tone. However, the ludicrousness of any pigs living in a farmhouse and in particular of Animal Farm's pigs living in the farmhouse, which, to top it all, had been declared by themselves a museum at the start of the novel, indicates the irony with which Orwell is presenting events. The word 'suddenly' helps us to detect Orwell's critical attitude towards the event. Similarly, when Orwell writes that after Napoleon's objections to the windmill, the animals were 'somewhat' surprised to learn that the windmill was to be built after all, we recognise the understatement in his use of the word 'somewhat', which contributes to the ironic tone.

Another example is when Orwell describes the animals' reactions to Snowball's windmill plans which, he writes, 'the other animals found completely unintelligible but very impressive'. By using the adverbs 'completely' and 'very' to qualify the contrasting adjectives 'unintelligible' and 'impressive', Orwell exaggerates the stupidity of the animals, creating humour and suggesting his ironic attitude towards the way politicians use knowledge to gain power.

Similarly, when Orwell writes that 'About this time there occurred a strange incident which hardly anyone was able to understand' (H68), words such as 'strange' and 'hardly anyone' suggest the irony with which he is writing.

At the end of the novel, the irony is clear when the final commandment is changed to a nonsensical statement in which the very meaning of equality is changed ('All animals are equal but some animals are more equal than others'). What Orwell seems to be saying here is that language has no purpose or meaning other than to serve the means of those in power.

Imagery

While Orwell's language appears simple, he does use imagery and is idiomatic in places, with language being used in metaphorical ways. For example, Orwell describes the neighbouring farmers as having 'changed their tune', meaning that they contradicted what they had previously said, and Mollie taking 'to her heels', meaning that she was running away. Also, Squealer is described as being able to 'turn black into white', which is of course not literal — it just means that he is very persuasive and can make the other animals believe anything he says.

The opening page offers us an example of personification when Orwell describes the light from Mr Jones's lantern as 'dancing from side to side' to suggest the unsteady movements of its owner. Later, in Chapter 5, Orwell uses a simile to describe the earth: it is 'like iron', conveying its hardness and the difficulties that face the animals. He also talks of the animals working 'like slaves', suggesting the cruel monotony of their exploitation. It is these choice details that help to create the atmosphere of pain. In some cases, hope is also conveyed in this way: 'The grass and the bursting hedges were gilded by the level rays of the sun' (H54). Here Orwell's use of a metaphor based on gold and hence relating to the metaphorical 'golden future time' mentioned in the song 'Beasts of England' helps to convey the idyllic image of a utopia that the animals hoped to achieve, in stark contrast to the harsh reality that they have just encountered with the killing of animals.

Propaganda: the power of language

Orwell also presents us with imagery through the inclusion of the propagandist song 'Beasts of England'. The references to 'golden future time' and

'fruitful fields of England' present us with metaphors of hope, in contrast to the symbols of tyranny encapsulated in the objects listed in the third verse. Here Orwell uses alternate rhyme, set rhythm and a refrain with the repeated first and last verses to signify the memorable anthem of hope for the animals, which the pigeons try to spread to neighbouring farms.

While its replacement also includes rhythm and rhyme, Orwell deliberately makes it brief, just two short lines: 'Animal Farm, Animal Farm/ Never through me shalt thou come to harm!' (H56). As a result, it lacks the idyllic vision and imagery presented in the original animals' song and shows the way that the regime has abandoned the ideals of the Rebellion.

It is only when Minimus is employed to write a propagandist poem about Napoleon that we see a return to the use of metaphor, this time in praise of the dictator, metaphorically describing Napoleon as the source of joy: the 'fountain of happiness' (H58). After presenting us with the reality of life on the farm, Orwell shows us the irony of propaganda. Given all that has happened, to compare Napoleon's eye to the 'sun in the sky' makes a mockery of the original ideals of Animalism. Similarly, to suggest that the animals' souls are on fire with its implied associations of joy highlights the poem's words as meaningless. Thus Orwell shows us the way in which politicians use language for their own ends.

Throughout the novel, we see how language is used by characters to gain power over others. This is explored more in the *Themes* section of this book.

Comedy

In addition to the ironic tone of the book, Orwell creates situational comedy. We may laugh at Mollie's depiction as vain, when we imagine a horse admiring herself in a mirror while holding a blue ribbon against her shoulder, or we might find Snowball's excitement over the windmill comical when he is depicted as holding his book open while gripping 'a piece of chalk' 'between the knuckles of his trotter' and uttering 'whimpers of excitement'. Orwell's carefully chosen words help to create vivid images of funny moments. A good example is found at the end of the novel when Orwell writes of Mr Pilkington's 'various chins' turning purple, which helps to convey a clear picture of the character's appearance and personality in a comical way.

We are meant to laugh at the image of pigs getting drunk on whisky and Napoleon's contradictory statements (typical of someone with a hangover) when he bans alcohol only to later look into brewing and distilling, for these comic moments ridicule the hypocrisy of the pigs as leaders and help Orwell to expose the truth behind what he saw as fascist regimes that masqueraded as socialism.

Grade *focus*

Questions on style are not as common as those on character and theme, although parts of questions can focus on the way in which language and structure are used by the writer to create effects. It is more likely that you will need to incorporate some material about style into your response in order to cover specific Assessment Objectives. Look at the details relating to AO2 and AO3 in the *Assessment Objectives and skills* section.

Review your learning

(Answers available online)

1. Why would it be accurate to describe *Animal Farm* as a satire?
2. Events in the novel represent historical occurrences and some characters relate to real people, so what sort of a story is *Animal Farm*?
3. What narrative voice is used in the novel?
4. What three adjectives might you use to describe the style of *Animal Farm*?

More interactive questions and answers online.

Tackling the assessments

- **What assessments will you face?**
- **How will your assessments be marked?**
- **What sorts of questions will you face?**
- **How can you prepare for your assessment?**
- **How can you plan your response?**
- **How can you structure your response?**
- **How can you ensure the best grade?**

Assessments

Depending on what board and specification you are following, you may have to respond to *Animal Farm* in an English Literature examination or Controlled Assessment, so knowing the text well is very important. The sort of response you will make in a Controlled Assessment may be written or multi-modal (a combination of written and spoken).

Literature

If you are studying towards Literature GCSE with AQA, Edexcel or OCR, then *Animal Farm* is an option either as part of your exam or a Controlled Assessment. The following table explains which unit the novel appears in and gives you information about the sort of question you will get and whether you can take your text into the exam or Controlled Assessment.

AQA	AQA	Edexcel	OCR
Unit 4: Approaching Shakespeare and the English Literary Heritage: Section B	Unit 3: The Significance of Shakespeare and the English Literary Heritage	Unit 1: Understanding Prose: Section A	Unit A664: Literary Heritage Prose and Contemporary Poetry
A written response in an exam to one out of two questions based on the whole text	A written or multi-modal response to a task set by AQA based on Themes and Ideas or Characterisation and Voice linking two texts	A four-part question linked to an extract in an exam	A written response to an exam consisting of either a passage-based question or a question requiring comment, criticism and analysis

AQA	AQA	Edexcel	OCR
Unannotated text allowed	Unannotated text allowed; dictionary and thesaurus as well as brief notes also allowed	Unannotated text allowed	Unannotated text allowed
30 minutes	3–4 hours	52.5 minutes	45 minutes
24 marks	40 marks	40 marks	16/24 marks

Marking

The marking of your responses varies according to the board and options your school or you have made. If you are studying *Animal Farm* for examination, an external examiner will mark your response, but if you are responding to it in a Controlled Assessment, your teacher will mark your work and it will then be moderated by someone else. In all cases, your ability to respond to the novel in a critical way is important. Assessment Objectives for individual assessments are explained in the next section of this guide.

Essay writing

Whether you are responding in an exam or Controlled Assessment, knowing how to plan, structure and write an essay is important. You are probably familiar with essay writing so you should have some idea about how to go about writing an essay but a few helpful tips are:

- Write in the present tense when you analyse texts.
- Only use the past tense when referring to a historical or social fact from the past.
- Address the question immediately.
- Provide evidence for your statements.
- Link your paragraphs.

Essay structure

Essays are made up of three sections: introduction, main body and conclusion.

Introduction

The introduction is made up of three or four sentences directed at the question. You could use the question as a lead and outline the main ideas you will cover in your essay. Look at the following example introduction written in response to a typical AQA question.

How does Orwell explore ideas about power in the novel?

Power is a key theme in the novel, through which Orwell explores the way that characters gain control over others to elevate their status and enrich their own lives. Significant characters who contribute to this exploration are Mr Jones, whom Orwell uses to represent tsarist Russia (in particular Tsar Nicholas II), and the pigs, who symbolise the Russian revolutionaries who became corrupted by power, abandoning the Rebellion's ideals for position and status.**1**

1 The candidate immediately addresses the question in the first sentence and then indicates the areas that will form the basis of the rest of the essay

Grade ***booster***

Avoid beginning your essay by spelling out exactly what you intend to do ('In this essay I will show that...'): just get on with it.

Main body

This is the central part of the essay and is usually formed of at least three and up to five or six paragraphs. Each paragraph deals with a different point and is linked to the previous paragraph.

The conclusion

The conclusion is your summing up of the evidence and your final words. It should restate main points but throw a new light on the subject, rather than just repeat the introduction. An example might be:

By the end of the novel, Orwell's political message is clear.**1** We are left in no doubt about the fact that as Lord Acton put it, 'power corrupts and absolute power corrupts absolutely'.**2** The last sentence in the novel leaves us with an uncomfortable awareness of the sad state of affairs in which ideals have been forgotten and comrades betrayed — where man and pig are now indistinguishable.**3**

1 A clear statement starting the conclusion of the essay. The word 'political' is key.

2 A second sentence reinforcing the opening one, referring back to the question and the key theme in the essay (power), as well as indicating the impact that the novel has had and the writer's success in conveying his message

3 An implied reference to the structure of the novel and the movement from utopia to dystopia

Grade ***booster***

Your entire essay builds an argument based on evidence, like a lawyer in court arguing a case, so writing and structuring your essay well and providing evidence are very important.

Using PEE

When you write a paragraph in a critical essay, you should think of PEE: Point, Evidence, Explanation. Essentially this consists in making a statement, supporting it with evidence from the text (which may be a quotation) and then explaining how the evidence shows what you said in your statement. It is a good idea to embed your quotation, in other words to put it into your own sentence (rather than citing it after a colon) as this is a sign of a higher-level candidate. It is also a good idea to link your explanation to the question you are answering, so that you stay on track. Here is an example.

We are aware of power structures on the farm in the first chapter.**1** It is evident that a hierarchy between the animals exists, with old Major sitting on a 'raised platform' and the dogs and pigs sitting immediately in front of him in the barn.**2** By describing the animals sitting in this way, Orwell signals the way in which, despite efforts at equality, the pigs and dogs will later assume the dominant roles on the farm.**3**

1 The statement

2 The evidence (an embedded quotation within a description)

3 The explanation, where the candidate analyses particular words or references, explaining how they support the statement and then links the essay back to the question. This is a very good example of using PEE.

Grade *booster*

To check how good you are at embedding quotations, read your sentences out to someone who has not read the novel. See if they can tell where Orwell's words begin and end. If not, you have integrated his words smoothly.

Developing an argument and linking paragraphs

Part of essay technique is making sure that the examiner or teacher knows that you are developing an argument. You can make this clear by using 'signal words' to signpost your argument.

Word/phrase	What it does
however, although, yet	Suggests an exception: **However**, we recognise the deception in what Squealer is saying.
nevertheless, nonetheless, despite this	Signals a contradiction: **Despite this**, Clover has no thought of rebellion.
similarly, likewise, in a similar way	Indicates a similarity: Boxer believes in the ideals of Animalism and works hard. **Similarly**, Clover never loses heart, until the very end of the novel.
in contrast, conversely, ... differs from..., while	Suggests a contrast or opposite idea: **Conversely**, Benjamin is able to recognise what is going on but he does not involve himself.

Word/phrase	What it does
moreover, furthermore, in addition	Builds on the previous point, making a stronger point: **Moreover**, in refusing to tell the animals what he can see, he allows evil to prevail.
above all	Introduces the most important point: **Above all**, the pigs not only deceive their fellow animals but betray the principles of Animalism.
in summary, in conclusion	Concludes the essay: **In conclusion**, through his allegorical tale, Orwell suggests that there is something in human nature that will always seek violence, conflict and power over others.

Grade *booster*

It is really important that you show an awareness of the novel as a constructed work. Make clear that you know that this is a novel and that the characters are constructs through which Orwell expresses his thoughts and ideas. To do this, you need to foreground the writer, using statements such as:

- Orwell highlights…
- The author makes clear…
- He elaborates…
- The author portrays…
- He illustrates…
- Orwell reinforces…
- He shows…
- He demonstrates…

Questions

The sorts of questions you will face in your exam and Controlled Assessment could be questions about characters, voice, themes, ideas, structure, the writer's intentions and the novel in context.

The Controlled Assessment questions are general ones that will be applied to *Animal Farm* by your teachers. Examples of questions for a Controlled Assessment are:

Explore how writers present the idea of change in two texts you have studied. (AQA-style Controlled Test)

Explore how two texts you have studied present characters who are exploited. (AQA-style Controlled Test)

Questions for an exam may be passage-based, formed of four parts or just one question. Examples of single passage-based questions for an exam are:

What role do you think the sheep and dogs hold in helping the pigs to maintain control over the animals? (AQA-style Literature higher-tier exam question)

How does Orwell use elements of satire to convey his ideas about society in *Animal Farm*? (AQA-style Literature higher-tier exam question)

Explore the ways in which Orwell presents *Animal Farm* as a fable. (AQA-style Literature higher-tier exam question)

How does Orwell develop sympathy for Boxer in two chapters of the novel? (OCR-style Literature higher-tier exam question)

What role do you think the sheep and dogs hold in helping the pigs to maintain control over the animals?
You should consider:

- what the sheep and dogs do in the novel and what they may represent
- when the sheep and dogs appear
- how they aid the pigs

(AQA-style Literature foundation-tier exam question)

How does Orwell develop sympathy for Boxer in two chapters of the novel?

- how Boxer is described
- what Boxer says and does
- how he is treated by others

(OCR-style Literature foundation-tier exam question)

Grade *booster*

Four-part questions may ask you to (a) summarise events in the passage, then (b) explain how the writer presents a certain theme, using evidence, then (c) state what you learn about a particular character, using evidence, then (d) explain how a particular character is presented/treated by exploring language. Prepare for these by making sure you know which themes especially relate to each character.

Preparation and planning

Preparing yourself for your assessment will involve a combination of rereading and revision of the text, research and essay practice. All

Pause for thought

A useful exercise in preparation for your essays is to:

1. Write down the key events of the novel.
2. Write a one-paragraph description of each of the major characters.
3. Write a brief summary of what the writer set out to do.

responses require you to write clearly, so focusing on writing skills and approaches to questions is important. If you have a choice of questions, then choosing the right question is an important part of getting a good mark.

Make sure you choose the question that you are able to answer best. Candidates often find character questions more straightforward than others but there are no set rules. The best thing is for you to get as much practice as possible in the types of questions you might face. This means planning and writing timed essays.

Identifying key words and planning ideas

Getting your essays to take shape requires you to write in a cohesive way. This means that you need to plan and organise your ideas and link your paragraphs.

First key word — question start

Whatever question you face, you need to consider what the question is asking you. Foundation-tier questions will help you by providing you with some bullet points, but if you are taking the higher-tier GCSE, then you will not get much guidance in terms of what areas to explore, so you will need to come up with a planned approach yourself.

A good way of doing this is to look at question starts and to identify the key words in the question. Questions often start with words like 'how', 'what', 'why' and 'who', but they can start in other ways too. Words such as 'what' and 'where' suggest straightforward retrieval of information. The word 'how', however, indicates the need to explain and analyse, and the word 'why' suggests that you need to give reasons. Questions that start with 'explore' suggest that a full discussion is required, and those that start with 'to what extent' or 'how far do you agree' are setting up a debate and asking you for your opinion. The first thing to do, then, is to read the start of the question carefully to know what is being asked of you.

Other key words

Next, identify the other key words, consider what each word means and implies, and then come up with ideas of what points you might include in your essay and what events you might refer to.

Organise your ideas — an example

Finally, you need to organise your ideas and decide on the order in which you will cover these.

Consider, for example, the question used earlier:

Because of the word 'how', you know that you need to explain and analyse, but you can also see that the other key words are 'explore', 'ideas' and 'power', so you would then consider each of these words.

The word 'explore' suggests that you need to look in detail at the different devices that Orwell uses in his novel, so recognising that the novel is a satire that makes comments about society and is an allegory for the Russian Revolution will help you here.

The word 'ideas' shows that it is not simply power that Orwell explores but other notions connected to it, so you would need to consider what exactly he is saying about power. Knowing that Orwell's experiences in the Spanish Civil War had shaped his views of communism in action and human interaction will help you respond to this.

Finally, the word 'power' suggests that you need to focus on the way in which Orwell presents power — which characters exercise power over others, how and why?

All this preliminary exploration of the question would give you a number of ideas for different points to make in your essay, such as:

- the novel as a satire
- the novel as an allegory
- the events in the novel and their corresponding historical events
- the characters in the novel who hold/do not hold power and their corresponding historical figures
- instances when characters use power

Your next stage of planning would be to organise these points according to where in your essay you would like them to appear. You might then jot down some events and quotations from the book to support each point. It would also be worth you thinking about any films you have seen and what you know of the context of the novel to see if any of this would help you support any points.

If this question were set at foundation tier, it could be worded as follows:

> How does Orwell explore ideas about power in the novel?
> Consider:
> - the way that Mr Jones and the pigs behave
> - how conditions on the farm change
> - the ending of the novel

If you were answering this question, you would use the bullet points to help guide you but you might also consider some of your own ideas. Remember to find events and quotations from the novel to support your ideas. Also think about how the novel is performed and the context of the novel to help make your answer as good as possible.

An example of a first paragraph in this essay might be:

> It is clear from the start that Jones has power over the animals as he is described as a 'hard master', and at the end of Chapter 1 he is able to easily silence the animals by firing his gun.**1** He is said by old Major to 'consume without producing' — just as any capitalist (whom he represents) does, and this is what we see the pigs begin to do as early as Chapter 3 when they are said to direct the others to work rather than work themselves.**2** This prepares us for the position of power that the pigs gradually assume.**3** Both they and Jones are used by Orwell to represent the most powerful in society — the aristocracy in tsarist Russia in Jones's case and the Russian Communist leaders in the case of the pigs.**4**

1 A strong topic sentence focused on the question with clear evidence and good knowledge of the book coming through

2 A comparison between Jones and the pigs that shows an awareness of themes, symbolism and satire

3 The point is developed and the candidate introduces the way the writer crafts his novel

4 This sentence refers to the novel's social and historical context, and shows that the candidate understands the allegorical structure of the text. Overall in this paragraph, embedded quotations, close reference to the novel and a clear style make the argument fluid, indicating a higher-level candidate. This is a very good response from an A* candidate.

Pause for thought

As a revision exercise, go through the six higher-tier questions on page 75 and suggest the bullet-point guidance you would expect to see if they were offered at the foundation tier. This is a useful activity whichever tier you are entered for. As you can see, higher-tier and foundation-tier questions are similar. The main difference is that foundation-tier candidates will generally receive more guidance about how to tackle the question.

Multi-modal responses

If you are doing the AQA Controlled Assessment and have opted to respond by both writing and presenting other evidence on the novel, you need to make sure that you prepare just as thoroughly as you would do for a full written response. You will have plenty of time to research so use it. The internet is a useful source of information, as is this guide. Follow the advice given above when thinking about your chosen question. Also, make sure that you organise your ideas and know what you will write and how you will support your statements using evidence from video clips, websites or films.

Even though you will be presenting information in a different way, you still need to structure what you present in an organised way, using Standard English.

Grade *booster*

If the meaning of a question seems unclear or too open to interpretation, consider choosing another question if there is a choice. If you still decide to tackle this question, make it clear what your interpretation of the question is.

Achieving an A*

In order to gain an A*, you have to respond with confidence and enthusiasm, exploring through well-selected quotations how the writer uses language and structure to create certain effects. You need to show sophisticated critical analysis and originality in your interpretations of the novel. You should show how the social and historical context affects how the novel was written and is received, and you need to shape your essay well.

Achieving a C

In order to gain a C, you need to show understanding and knowledge of how Orwell uses ideas, themes and setting to affect the reader. You should respond in a personal way to the effects of language and structure and use quotations to support what you say. You should show some awareness of the social and historical context of the novel and write clearly.

Review your learning

(Answers available online)

1. What is an essay?
2. How can you plan your answer?
3. How do you use PEE effectively?
4. Which words can you use in an essay to suggest contrast and which to suggest an exception?

More interactive questions and answers online.

Assessment Objectives and skills

- **What are Assessment Objectives?**
- **Which objectives will I be assessed on?**
- **What skills do I need to meet these objectives?**
- **How can I prepare for these Assessment Objectives?**

A teacher or examiner marks your piece of work based on whether you have fulfilled certain Assessment Objectives. In other words, they mark your work to see whether you have done certain things.

English Literature Assessment Objectives

The key Assessment Objectives that apply to your English Literature studies of *Animal Farm* are as follows:

- AO1
  - Respond to texts critically and imaginatively.
  - Select and evaluate relevant textual detail to illustrate and support interpretations.
- AO2
  - Explain how language, structure and form contribute to writers' presentation of ideas, themes and settings.
- AO3
  - Explain links between texts.
  - Evaluate writers' different ways of expressing meaning and achieving effects.
- AO4
  - Relate texts to their social, cultural and historical contexts.
  - Explain how texts have been influential and significant to self and other readers in different contexts and at different times.

The Assessment Objectives you need to address and the importance of each of these Assessment Objectives (AOs) vary across boards.

- For Edexcel, you must address AO1, AO2 and AO4, but more weighting is placed on AO1 and AO4 than on AO2.

- For AQA's Controlled Assessment, you must address AO1, AO2, AO3 and AO4, but more weighting is placed on AO2.
- For AQA's exam, you must address AO1, AO2 and AO4 but less weighting is placed on AO4.
- For OCR's exam, you must address AO1 and AO2 and OCR places equal importance on AO1 and AO2.

Now let us break down each AO to see what it means.

AO1

'Respond to texts *critically*': this means that you say what you think of the novel and explain why you think this. You are being asked to *analyse* the text as a piece of literature that has been created by a writer. You would be analysing if you showed that you understood how Orwell creates characters through:

- a combination of what characters say and do
- how they speak
- direct description

Discussing the way Orwell creates irony in the text would also show that you are analysing how the novel works.

'...and *imaginatively*': this means you do not simply repeat straightforward ideas. You need to know the text well enough to come up with your own interesting interpretations. You could do this by stating that Moses's depiction as a raven tamed by Jones is significant because he represents orthodox religion reconciling the poor and suffering to their lot in life; this depiction could reflect Orwell's view that the Church is often used by corrupt governments as a tame pet to help them maintain control over the populace by quelling any notions of rebellion.

'*Select* and *evaluate* relevant textual detail to illustrate and support interpretations': this means that you can find words, phrases and evidence from the novel to support the comments that you make. You are also able to explain the choices that the writer has made and *assess* how effective you think they are at contributing to the writer's intentions. For example, you might use the fact that Orwell shows Boxer adopting the motto of 'I will work harder' to show that he is a loyal and committed worker, representing the proletariat in Russia, and his second motto of 'Napoleon is always right' to indicate his unquestioning obedience to the leadership. You might then evaluate what Orwell is saying about such obedience, when Boxer is cruelly killed by the pigs for a crate of whisky.

AO2

***'Explain how* language, structure and form contribute to writers' presentation of ideas, themes and settings'**: this means that you show how the words that Orwell uses and the way he has shaped and organised his novel have helped him to convey certain ideas and messages and to create a setting. This area is covered closely in the *Style* section of this guide. You might discuss the way Orwell uses repetition to suggest the deteriorating conditions on the farm, for example.

AO3

'Explain links between texts': this means that you draw comparisons between two texts that have similar themes. Recognising that both *The Tempest* and *Animal Farm* present us with ideas of utopian/dystopian worlds would be an example of this.

'Evaluate writers' different ways of expressing meaning and achieving effects': this means that you analyse how writers use characters, language, imagery, genre, structure and so on to achieve their aims. Exploring the way in which Orwell uses animals and Shakespeare uses magical characters to convey themes and attitudes, and discussing the extent to which these work would show that you are addressing this objective.

AO4

***'Relate* texts to their social, cultural and historical contexts'**: this means that you know what events Orwell based his novel on and what influenced his writing. For example, you understand the parallels between the way the humans and later the pigs treat the animals and how this corresponds with the way that the Romanov dynasty and the corrupt Communist regime treated the Soviet citizens. Also your knowledge of Orwell's own views about politics and his experiences in the Spanish Civil War will help you to address this AO. This is covered extensively in the *Context* section of this book.

***'Explain how* texts have been influential and significant to self and other readers in different contexts and at different times'**: this means that you can show how you have responded personally to the novel and how it still holds meaning for you and for others. In other words, you can explain how it is still relevant today and has been and would be relevant at different times throughout history. For example, the novel can still be seen as relevant because it deals with issues that we still face, such as capitalism, power and, as Orwell said, 'man's dominion over' others. In fact it is even more relevant now, given the commercialism of the modern

> **Grade *booster***
>
> Make sure you write the names of the novel and characters correctly. Also use quotation marks around the name of the book and words taken from the text.

world. The exploitation of people and of animals is still relevant today, with issues such as slave and child labour appearing in the news and dictators still existing in some countries.

How you can prepare

- Know the novel well.
- Find out exactly what is required of you in the exam or Controlled Assessment.
- Understand the novel properly and be able to discuss key ideas in detail.
- Be able to support your comments and explore how Orwell creates meaning and effects.
- Read around the subject and look into the background of the novel.
- Watch film versions of the novel.
- Look at plenty of example exam questions and have a go at some.
- Remind yourself of the key Assessment Objectives and make sure you know how to address these.
- Ask your teacher for help if you need to.

Grade *booster*

Make sure you write in an appropriate way in your exam. Although it is your understanding of the novel and not the way you write that is being assessed, you must write clearly and formally.

- Do not use slang or colloquial language, except when you are quoting from the novel. For example, do not write 'the pigs do in Boxer'.
- Use appropriate critical vocabulary, for example 'convey', 'portray', 'demonstrate', 'devices' and 'technique'.

What you will not gain marks for

The AOs guide you towards what you need to write; they tell you what will gain you marks. However, it is also important to know that you will *not* gain marks for the following:

- **Retelling the story.** Examiners already know what *Animal Farm* is about. You will not gain any credit for telling them what they already know and what they assume you already know. You must answer the question you are asked and address the AOs, not write down everything you know about the story — that would be a waste of your time.

- **Using very long quotations.** You need to quote from the novel to support what you write, but quoting long sections will not gain you marks. It wastes your time and just shows that you are not able to select the quotation you need. It is much better to quote short phrases and words or, even better, to embed quotations into your sentences.
- **Giving your opinion in a dismissive way without any support.** The examiner wants to see that you have responded personally to a text, so writing your opinion is a good thing but only if it makes sense and you have supported what you write with evidence from the text or elsewhere. Rather than writing 'Napoleon's a really mean two-faced pig', write 'When Napoleon has Boxer killed and then organises a banquet in his honour, drinking whisky from the proceeds of his sale, we see that he is a cruel and hypocritical character.'
- **Identifying features.** It is good that you are able to recognise when a character is using a rhetorical question or is being emotive or when there is a comic moment in the novel, but it is not enough just to recognise these features. You should not just write: 'Squealer uses rhetorical questions when he talks to the animals.' You need to be able to explain why Orwell has characters use these devices and how they work in creating certain effects, so you should write: 'Orwell uses rhetorical questions and emotive language when Squealer explains away Napoleon taking on the leadership of the farm. By using the words "...and then where should we be?" he shows how the manipulation of language by those in power can influence others. Here Squealer makes the animals question their own judgement and by using the exaggerated and emotive metaphor of "moonshine" to describe Snowball's idea of a windmill, he mocks it, suggesting that it was an impossible and foolish dream, thus distancing the animals from it. Orwell was concerned with the way in which language and power related; through Squealer, he presents the voice of propaganda and shows the influence it can have.'

Grade *booster*

Make sure you read the question properly. You need to answer all parts of the question.

Review your learning

(Answers available online)

1. What AOs will you be assessed on for English Literature?
2. Give two examples of something that would not get you marks.
3. Give an example of how you would address AO4.

More interactive questions and answers online.

Sample essays

- **What does the beginning of an essay look like?**
- **How do I write a character essay?**
- **How do I write a theme-based essay?**
- **What makes a good essay?**

Essay questions and some samples were provided in the *Tackling the assessments* section of this book. Below you will find some more extracts from sample essays, with examiner comments.

Look at the C-grade responses and try to improve these. Then look at the A-grade responses and compare them to your own ideas. Although there is no set way of approaching an answer, the higher-level responses will help you in answering questions yourself.

Essay beginnings

Remember to begin your essay by immediately focusing on the question. You should use the question as a lead and outline the main ideas you will cover in your essay. This was tackled in the *Tackling the assessments* section, so refer back for more guidance.

How does Orwell use the pigs to suggest the way in which power corrupts? (AQA Literature)

Grade-C response — beginning

I'm going to write about how Orwell uses the pigs to suggest the way power corrupts.**1** The pigs are greedy animals who want more and more. Napoleon is very power-hungry and gets rid of Snowball to get power.**2** Power corrupts Napoleon because he starts to break commandments and he betrays ideals.**3**

1 Immediate focus on question but says what will be done rather than just doing it

2 Knowledge of the pigs' natures and in particular the most dominant pig is seen, as is knowledge of a key event

3 The candidate knows about the fact that commandments are broken but does not elaborate on this and refers to ideals but does not exemplify these, making clear how this shows corruption, so AO1 is not covered well

This response is a C-grade one because understanding and knowledge of the novel are shown by the candidate and these are focused on the question. However, statements imply understanding of how the pigs are corrupt rather than showing it with proper evidence. Also, although this starts quite well and is focused on the question, it is not advisable to say what you will do.

Grade-A response — beginning

Animal Farm is a satire in which Orwell uses the pigs to expose the way in which socialist governments deteriorate into fascist regimes that manipulate others to gain and maintain power.**1** Orwell based his novel on events in Russia and on his experiences in the Spanish Civil War, where he saw the way in which power corrupted people to betray the ideals upon which they had created the government. In the same way, Orwell presents the pigs as betraying the ideals of Animalism — a system of government based on old Major's speech in Chapter 1.**2** The pigs and in particular Napoleon are presented as powerful from the start, when they sit at the front of the barn in Chapter 1 and when Napoleon is described as having a 'reputation for getting his own way'. Later, when he consumes the milk, we see that he places his needs above those of the rest of the farm.**3** This prepares us for the way in which he starts to break the Seven Commandments, which eventually leads to their complete erosion.**4**

1 Immediate focus on the question; shows understanding of the genre and context of the novel as well as Orwell's political intentions

2 Use of specific references to the text and parallel between real events and the novel, showing good understanding of context again

3 Explains how Orwell's choices help us to see the power of the pigs, using close reference to the text

4 Analyses the effect these choices have on us and links the analysis to the question

This response is an A-grade one because of the confidence with which the candidate writes about the novel and the way the paragraph is very clearly linked to the question. Understanding and interpretation of the novel and its context (AO4) are shown by the candidate, who has referred to well-selected evidence as well as Russian history and has embedded quotations (AO1). The candidate's awareness of Orwell as a writer is clear as she explains how he makes choices to show the main theme of the novel (AO2).

This candidate continued in this very focused way when she discussed, later in her essay, the part that language plays in maintaining power:

Orwell shows us the way that the pigs maintain power over the animals using language, for example when some of the animals do not understand the words 'propulsion' and 'manipulation' that Snowball uses but accept his explanation, suggesting their lack of power.**5** Similarly when Squealer later manipulates the animals into accepting Snowball's expulsion from the farm and Napoleon's sudden adoption of the windmill project, he describes this as 'tactics' — a word they are unfamiliar with.**6** It is this complication of language, along with rhetorical questions and emotive language, that enable Squealer to pacify the animals**7** and that help Orwell to show the way in which Communist Russia used propaganda to maintain power over the masses.**8**

5 A point is made; the candidate links this paragraph to the question by restating the theme of power; evidence is provided and analysed (AO1 and AO2)

6 A second example is provided to reinforce the point made (AO1)

7 The candidate analyses the devices used by Squealer (AO2)

8 Links events to history, showing knowledge of context (AO4)

Character questions

Character questions are common in assessments and some students find these easier to tackle. Be prepared to answer a question that asks you to consider the following:

- the importance of one of the characters
- whether a character has changed or developed during the novel
- whether a character has learned anything by the end of the novel
- similarities or differences between characters in the novel
- whether a character is sympathetic or not
- whether we sympathise with a character
- how the writer shapes a character
- how the writer wants us to react to a character

An example of a character question is:

How does Orwell develop sympathy for Boxer in two chapters of the novel? Consider:

- how Boxer is described
- what Boxer says and does
- how others react to Boxer and anything else you think is relevant

(OCR-style Literature foundation-tier exam question)

Grade-C response

Orwell makes us feel sorry for Boxer in two chapters because we see him being treated badly by the pigs.**1** Benjamin's reaction shows us how badly he is treated: 'Fools! Do you not see what is written on the side of that van?'**2** Boxer is a kind horse who works hard so we get to like him and we are shocked that he is killed.**3** When we find out that the pigs sell him we see how bad the pigs really are and we feel very sorry for him as a result.**4**

1 Focus on the question; awareness of Orwell as a writer (AO2) but implies that the only time we have sympathy for Boxer is in two chapters

2 Quotation indirectly shows how Orwell creates sympathy but this is not fully explained

3 Summarises Boxer's qualities and recognises our reactions but does not provide specific evidence to support the statements made, so AO1 is not covered well

4 This is more specific and shows knowledge of the text but is explained too simply and not developed

Grade-A response

The way that Boxer is presented by Orwell gains our and the other animals' admiration. He is described as 'an enormous beast' upon whom the farm relies.**1** We recognise his 'unfailing' commitment to Animalism, despite his inability to understand it fully, and we see his loyalty and dedication to the farm in the way that he arranges with the cockerel to be wakened earlier than the others.**2** His personal mottos of 'I will work harder' and 'Napoleon is always right' make him an endearing character for us, but the two chapters where Orwell makes us feel most sympathy are Chapters Six and Nine.**3**

1 Clear focus on the question

2 Evidence is provided with direct quotation and close reference to the text (AO1)

3 More evidence is provided and analysed (AO2); clear focus on the specific chapters that will form the basis of the essay

This is a strong opening paragraph and warrants a high grade, at least a B. The candidate makes good use of the bullet points given in

the question to help structure his response. While context (AO4) is not assessed with OCR, later inclusion and awareness of the text as a satire would secure an A grade.

Theme questions

Some questions focus on themes. You might get a question that asks you to consider one of the following:

- the presentation of a theme in the novel
- how the theme influences events in the novel
- how a theme is evident through the behaviour of one or more characters
- how the importance of a theme is evident

An example of a theme-based question is:

> The novel focuses on the difference between ideal and real worlds. Explain. (AQA-style higher-tier exam question)

This question is about the themes of utopia and dystopia (as discussed in the *Themes* section of this book).

Grade-C response

Animal Farm is based on an ideal which goes wrong.**1** Old Major explains this ideal in his speech and the song that the animals sing shows this ideal. The song says 'for that day we all must labour', meaning that the animals need to work towards this ideal of animals ruling themselves.**2** The farm is built around this ideal and the rules show this.**3** When the pigs start to break the rules we know that the real world is starting to come into play.**4**

1 Focus on the question; shows understanding of what the book is essentially about (AO1)

2 Knowledge of the text and reference to key symbols and incidents are noted but not naming the song suggests that the knowledge of the book is a little vague; although the candidate quotes from the song, the line choice does not provide sufficient scope for development and the explanation is general

3 Again some knowledge of the text is shown but remains vague

4 Shows understanding of how the ideal world is corrupted by the pigs but the reference again to rules rather than commandments is simplistic and the expression is not as precise as it could be; AO2 not addressed well and as yet AO4 not addressed

Grade-A response

In *Animal Farm*, Orwell explores the difference between ideal and real through his presentation of life post-Rebellion. Life after the Rebellion is initially based on old Major's utopian ideals, but later life comes under Napoleon's rule and becomes a dystopian nightmare, akin to the extremes of a totalitarian government.**1** Orwell drew much of his material from Russian history and his experiences in the Spanish Civil War; this is apparent in the first chapter when we see parallels between old Major and figures such as Marx and Lenin. The

1 Strong focus on the question with an indication of how Orwell shows the difference between ideal and real; clear reference to the book and its political basis (AO1, AO4)

system that the animals create, based on old Major's speech, is named Animalism and has links with socialism in its call for equality and collective ownership.**2** Orwell emphasises the wonder of this post-Rebellion world and presents it as idyllic when he describes the animals waking to a new 'dawn' and looking around in the 'clear morning light', implying the spiritual and pure nature of this world. He describes the animals leaping 'with excitement' and being in 'ecstasy' as if 'they had never seen these things before', emphasising their utter joy at recognising that the farm was 'all their own' and no longer Jones's.**3** By doing this, Orwell makes clear the way in which the animals are experiencing the ideal that is described in the song 'Beasts of England', which refers to a 'golden future time'.**4**

2 Clear development of the first point, demonstrating a strong understanding of the novel in context (AO4)

3 Exploration of Orwell's techniques in presenting the ideal world, with some analysis (AO2); well-embedded quotations (AO1)

4 Further point showing close textual knowledge and a strong link to the question (AO1 and AO2)

Other questions

You could face other kinds of questions, such as four-part questions if you are sitting an Edexcel exam, or comparison questions if you are doing a Controlled Assessment on the text.

An example of a four-part question for Edexcel is:

Remind yourself of events from page 40, 'Once again the animals were conscious of...' to page 41, '...they had been mistaken.'
Answer all parts of the questions that follows as fully as you can:

(a) Outline the key events from when Mollie disappeared up to this extract. (10)
(b) Explain how the writer presents the theme of memory in this extract. (10)
(c) From this extract, what do you learn about the character Napoleon? Use evidence from the extract to support your answer. (8)
(d) The animals work hard and trust the leaders. Explain how they are treated later in the novel. (12)

(Edexcel-style higher-tier exam question)

For this sort of question you need to note the marks per sub-question and make sure you answer all parts.

Grade-C response

(a) After Mollie disappears, work on the farm is difficult. Snowball comes up with a plan for a windmill but Napoleon does not like it and even when he paints it on the floor Napoleon just pees on it. On the Sunday when the animals are going to vote, Snowball speaks and Napoleon says a few things but then gets his dogs to attack Snowball and he runs away. Napoleon takes charge and decides to start trading with other farms.

This response answers the question but the first sentence makes it sound as though Mollie's absence makes work on the farm difficult when she is in fact a shirker. The candidate also omits a couple of key events: the animals' shock at Snowball's expulsion and Napoleon's adoption of the windmill. It also does not cover what Napoleon saw as important: farm security and getting weapons. The response shows understanding (AO1) but needs a bit more detail, therefore warrants only a C grade.

(b) Squealer makes the animals think that there never was a rule about trade. He says that it was probably a lie Snowball made up. He makes the animals think that they have bad memories by asking them for proof in writing. The animals cannot write or read so he is tricking them and making them think they imagined the rule. Napoleon also makes sure the animals do not remember anything by talking over them and getting the sheep to bleat 'Four legs good, two legs bad!'

Again, the response answers the question but misses out a few details such as the dogs' influence and Squealer's clever use of questions to make the animals doubt themselves. Although a quotation is used as evidence, it does not directly relate to the theme of memory. Again, while understanding is shown, the lack of detail and elaboration means that the candidate has not evaluated textual details (AO1) well, so this is a C-grade response.

(c) Napoleon is a bully and all the animals are scared of him. We know this because the four pigs talk 'timidly'. Also the word 'abolished' means banned so Napoleon forces the animals to do things his way. He has a lot of control. We know this because when he raises his trotter for silence he gets it. He is very set on getting his own way and just ignores what the animals say. He ends his speech with 'Long live Animal Farm!' but what he really means is long live Napoleon.

The response is focused on the question and uses evidence from the extract to substantiate points. The clear focus on Orwell's words with explanation is a positive attribute of this response (AO2). The second half of the response includes some accurate points but no clear explanation, so while this response overall is better than a C, it is probably just a low B.

(d) The animals do work hard and are described as working 'like slaves'. They are lied to by the pigs. We see this here in the extract when Squealer lies about the rule on trade and later this continues. Later, the commandments change and the pigs take over, not letting the animals have any freedom. They are treated really badly.

The response is focused on the question but the candidate has rushed. This part of the question is worth 12 marks but the candidate has written very little. Also, the only references to later in the novel are general, suggesting that the candidate is not as familiar with the rest of the text as needed. This is a low grade D response.

Overall, taking all four parts into account, the response comes out as a C grade. AO1 has been addressed and so has AO2, but the heavily weighted AO4 has not.

Grade-A response

(a) After Mollie disappears, no one talks of her again. Her disappearance is akin to the way in which Russians defected to the West in search of a better life. Work on the farm is difficult and the pigs take to making all decisions as they consider themselves to be the cleverest animals. Snowball has studied Jones's old books and makes a number of suggestions to improve the farm, but Napoleon and Snowball can never agree. One of these suggestions is for a windmill which Snowball says will help the animals by producing electricity. He develops careful plans but Napoleon is not in favour of the windmill and wants to secure the farm using weapons instead. The animals are divided as to which way to turn. When Snowball chalks his plan on the shed floor, Napoleon shows his contempt for it by urinating on it. On the Sunday when the animals are set to vote, Snowball speaks eloquently about the windmill, convincing the animals to vote for him. Napoleon says very little but then he makes a strange whimpering noise and nine great dogs chase Snowball off the farm. Napoleon takes charge and announces the end of Sunday meetings — the pigs will make all decisions and there will be no more debates. Snowball is said to be a traitor and later Napoleon adopts the plans to build a windmill, which Squealer says he only 'seemed' to oppose. Work is hard and when resources run low, Napoleon decides to start trading with neighbouring farmers.

This response answers the question fully. It outlines the key events and relates some to the social and historical context (AO1 and AO4).

(b) The theme of memory is shown in this extract when Orwell writes that the animals were 'conscious of a vague uneasiness', indicating that they remembered something about a rule against trade. Orwell uses a question to suggest the fading recollections of the animals: '—had not these been among the earliest resolutions passed...?' The fact that the animals are described as *thinking* that they remembered indicates the doubt with which they view their memories. These doubts are what Squealer feeds on when he asks them questions: 'Are you certain...?', 'Have you any record...?', 'Is it written down anywhere?' Squealer plays on the animals' uncertainties and this, combined with their inability to read or write well, allows him to manipulate them into accepting what he says as truth. He uses a combination of questions and assertions to ensure that the animals' minds are set 'at rest', as Orwell says. Orwell uses Squealer to show how dictators and in particular the Communist regime under Stalin used propaganda to control their citizens. Napoleon also ensures that questions over past events are squashed when he raises his trotter for silence, deflects attention away from the matter at hand with reassurances that he will liaise with Whymper, and has the dogs growl

and sheep bleat out their maxim. These tactics ensure that the situation is controlled and proceedings follow the course that Napoleon wants them to. In this way, Orwell shows how the animals' memory and thoughts are controlled by the pigs, in the same way that fascist regimes control and manipulate the masses.

The response answers the question, showing critical and imaginative selection of evidence, which is analysed and evaluated well (AO1). The way in which Orwell uses language to present the theme of memory is also explored and the text's social and historical context is explained, the candidate showing clear understanding of Orwell's intentions (AO4).

c) Napoleon is presented as an unfeeling and single-minded dictator. We can see this in the language that Orwell uses to describe him and others' reactions to him. He is said to have 'abolished the meetings', suggesting that he forces things to happen. He is not one to discuss and come to a compromise. The way in which the pigs raise their voices 'timidly' shows that they fear him. Napoleon uses the dogs and sheep to ensure that he gets his own way. The dogs scare the animals and the sheep drown them out so that Napoleon is then able to railroad the animals by telling them that he has already organised everything for trading with neighbouring farms. Orwell pokes fun at the way that Napoleon suggests that he is making a sacrifice when he describes his contact with Whymper as a 'burden' which Napoleon has taken on.

The response is focused on the question and uses evidence from the extract to substantiate points (AO1). It is well expressed and clear analysis is present. The clear focus on Orwell's words, with evaluation and awareness of the writer's intentions (AO2), are positive attributes of this response.

(d) The animals work 'like slaves' trying to build the windmill. This they do several times: they do it once, then do it again after a storm knocks it down, and then a third time after some of Frederick's men attack the farm and blow up the windmill. The animals continue to work hard despite reductions in rations, although Squealer refers to these as 'readjustments'. Orwell shows the way in which the animals are fooled into believing that their food is not cut through clever manipulation of language. The animals continue to believe in the ideals of Animalism despite the gradual erosion of the commandments, with the pigs adopting more and more human traits. In Chapter 7, when several animals are forced to confess crimes and are killed, we see events through Clover's eyes and here Orwell allows us a brief insight into her thoughts, troubled by the fact that their ideals have been ruined: 'These scenes of terror and slaughter were not what they had looked forward to…' However, Orwell makes clear that she, as a representative of all the animals, still believes that she is 'far better off than they had been in the days of Jones', suggesting the blind commitment she has to the ideals of Animal Farm. When Orwell writes that she 'lacked the words to express' her thoughts, we are reminded of the way that the animals' thoughts are controlled by the pigs. By the end of the novel, few animals can remember what it was like before the Rebellion, and 'so far as they knew' it 'was as it had always been'. However, Orwell makes clear to us that 'somehow' the farm had grown richer without the animals benefiting, indicating his satirical stance. When at the end of the novel we hear Napoleon turning his back on the foundations of Animalism and Orwell points out that the pigs and men are indistinguishable, we see the way in which the pigs have been fully corrupted by power. Outside, the animals watch, unspeaking: they have been betrayed by their leaders but are mute in response, in the same way that oppressed citizens in a totalitarian state are unable to escape their oppression.

The response is focused on the question, showing critical analysis and selection and evaluation of material (AO1). Language and structure — with the reference to satire — are explained (AO2). Understanding of the social and historical context of the novel is also apparent (AO4). This part of the question is worth 12 marks and requires reference to the rest of the novel; the candidate has written enough and shown a close knowledge of the rest of the novel to warrant an A grade here.

Overall, all Assessment Objectives have been addressed well in all parts of the question. As a result, the candidate has gained a strong A grade.

Review your learning

(Answers available online)

1. What sorts of character questions might you face?
2. What sorts of theme questions could you face?
3. What is the best way to start an essay?
4. In four-part questions, what must you make sure that you do?

More interactive questions and answers online.